Livin' in the Mortuary

PUBLISHED BY
OUR WRITTEN LIVES OF HOPE, LLC

Our Written Lives of Hope provides publishing services for authors in various educational, religious, and human service organizations. For information, visit www.OurWrittenLives.com.

Copyright ©2016 Derrick Chatman
Author Photo and Cover Photos by Alonzoe Kyler
Cover Model Katrina Relaford
Cover & Interior Design by Our Written Lives

Library of Congress Cataloging-in-Publication Data
Chatman, Derrick 1964
Livin' in the Mortuary

Library of Congress Control Number: 2016914538
ISBN: 978-1-942923-18-3 (paperback)

Livin' in the Mortuary

Derrick "DC" Chatman

Dedication

First of all, I want to dedicate this book to my mother, Cora Tillman Chatman Smith, who had an opportunity to read the first draft of the first 5 chapters before she went on to Heaven.

I'll never forget how hard she laughed at the comedy in the beginning of the book. My mother, along with her mother Lizzie Tillman, raised seven sons with no fathers, and none of her sons ever were arrested or went to jail. My mother worked two full time jobs as a nurse at both Fairview Park Hospital and May's Nursing Home to make sure we had the necessary things of life.

Additionally, they also kept three additional sons (The Burkes), and opened the doors of our home to so many folks who needed a safe family environment.

I also want to dedicate this book to my godmother, Essie Mae Relaford, who passed one week before my mother. Aunt Essie taught me so many things about life and the struggle of being dedicated to God rather than man.

We stayed up many late nights during my summers in Savannah, Georgia discussing the day's activities at the laundry mat. She gave me a lot of pointers concerning how to grow up as an honorable man with great values.

Contents

Chapter One

"Ashes to ashes, dust to dust," the preacher says on a hot sunny afternoon as he stands in the middle of Rosewood Cemetery in Macon, Georgia. The coffin is lowered into the ground, and then, suddenly, the handles break and the coffin falls directly into the grave! As the pallbearers look on in bewilderment, the preacher says, "AMEN!"

Gritting her teeth, Mother speaks to her daughter Azalea. "I told you to get a new coffin. Why are you burying your father in the coffin we used for the company's *display sign?*"

A funeral attendant turns and stares at the two women as they continue to scold each other. Azalea suddenly notices the man is watching them, so she lowers her head and pretends to cry.

"Because Daddy didn't order any new coffins when he got sick! That's why," Azalea snaps.

The preacher walks over and hugs Azalea and then her mother. The other mourners line up to greet the bereaved, but are distracted when blue lights from the Macon Police Department rush down Riverside Street in pursuit of a white van.

Azalea glances toward the sirens, and is practically knocked off of her feet as her aunt suddenly bear-hugs her. "Ahhhh! I can't breathe, T. Sister!"

Affectionately called T. Sister, Azalea's aunt is a hefty woman wearing a very large hat. She's weeping and wailing as she continues to squeeze the air out of Azalea. Seeing the commotion, three Sisters from the church rush over with funeral fans. They begin fanning and grabbing at Azalea. One Sister sticks smelling salt up Azalea's nose, which forces the poor girl to exhale deep breathes of air as she screams from the pain of the salts and T. Sister's grip.

With a weak voice, Azalea says, "Let–go-of-me . . . You cra-a-z-y woman!"

Shocked at what Azalea just said, T. Sister and her church ladies instantly stop crying and carrying on. "*What* did you say?" T. Sister asked, her eyes wide with surprise and suspicion. Her hat feathers flap as she jerks her head to the side, raising her eyebrows in preparation for a potential offense.

Irritated and exhausted, Azalea composes herself then pretends to cry again. "I said that I let go of him. I let go of Daddy. He was so crazy . . . *about his woman!* Praise the Lord! Boo-Hoo-Hoo!"

T. Sister and the church ladies instantly began to cry and grab Azalea again! This time, Azalea is forced to scream as she gasps for air and weeps in pain simultaneously!

"Oh, check on Momma! Ah, his woman! Check on my momma," she said as she tricks her aunt and the ladies into moving on down the receiving line toward her mother.

Mother looks at Azalea with widened "please save me" eyes as T. Sister grabs her in the bear-hug.

~ Change of Scene ~

"All units, be on the lookout for up to three males traveling south on Jeffersonville Road in a white van. Norest, Nevada tag number: D-A-K-3-6-9-L. Copy?" the police officer says as he follows in high-speed pursuit of the suspects.

"10-4. Back up is on the way," the 911 operator responds.

The high-speed chase runs directly into the congested traffic near the cemetery. The white van temporarily yields to the on-coming funeral procession. "I've got you now!" The officer says as he pulls up directly behind the white van.

Seeing the cop, the van driver darts between two of the limousines, which are carrying grieving family members. Blocked out, the police officer loses the chase. "Darn it!" He yells as he slams his hand on the steering wheel of his squad car.

~ Change of Scene ~

"Everybody, hold tight!" yells the limo-driver!

Azalea screams as a white van rushes toward the limousine she is riding in. A head-on collision is exactly what this day does *not* need. She can't imagine how horrible spending the night at the ER with her mother, aunts, and the church ladies would be. The past two hours were torture enough.

T. Sister and the church ladies are busy gossiping in the back of the limo. They don't see the close call, or hear the driver's warning. They do hear Azalea as she screams. Auntie and church ladies immediately stop talking, and turn to stare at Azalea.

"Oooh, Baby! T. Sister is here! Go ahead and let it out. You have to be strong for your mother," T. Sister says as she grabs Azalea in another unbearable-hug. Azalea screams.

"Bless your heart," says one of the church Sisters.

"Get the smelling salt," another says. The women begin their weeping as quickly as if they were turning on a water faucet.

Azalea begins crying for real this time as she endures the pain of her aunt's hug and the agony of the church ladies as they stick smelling salt up her nose.

~ Change of Scene ~

The white van speeds down Jeffersonville Highway, turns left, turns right, then turns left again onto US Highway 80 East, and keeps going for an hour. The driver pulls into an abandoned yard featuring a broken mailbox, rusty chair, and a dilapidated birdhouse. The van slams to a halt after pulling directly into an old car shelter at the back of the rundown house. The shelter almost crumbles on top of the van from the impact of the stop.

Yielding guns, two men jump out of the van and walk up to the house. A swing on the back porch hangs from a rusty chain. The seat is dusty, broken, and oddly designed—most likely homemade. They knock down the back door only to find a deserted room with dusty junk all over the place, and no electricity. They motion for a third person to join them. They make their way through the house, ducking as they peer through a broken glass window, hoping they were not followed.

"The coast is clear," a deep voice says. "We'll make ourselves at home and hide out for a while because we can't go back up to Chicago!"

Chapter Two

The funeral is over, and so is the dinner. Mother picks up empty plates from the coffee table in the living room. Azalea and the church ladies graciously clean up the additional mess visitors left in the dining room. T. Sister is busy in the kitchen, working her own assembly line, as she prepares ten 'to-go plates' for herself.

"Mattie, you don't need all of this food to spoil," T. Sister says to her sister, the widow. "I'll take some home with me, Baby. Don't you worry, and besides you know it ain't good for your ker-es-ta-raul. You know that's what took *your John* away from here."

Mattie almost drops the dishes she is carrying, but catches them mid-air. She pauses as she slowly places the plates into the sink. Everyone is silent.

"OK! Ahhhh! Take it with you. Take it all! Take it!" Azalea snaps at Auntie. "Thanks yall for coming!" She says as she begins to push the church ladies out of the kitchen through the living room to the front door.

Immediately protesting, the ladies shout.

"Oh, how ungrateful!"

"Oh, my! Huh!"

"Oh, I've NEVER!"

Azalea rolls her eyes. "Why am I NOT surprised?" She shouts back at the women. "But, um, thank you Aunties. Thank you. We appreciate everything, but, *my mother and me, we just need some time alone.*"

She continues to push the ladies out of the front door. T. Sister is holding her to-go plates in both arms. As Azalea slams the door, the plates smash together and squirt collard-green juice right into T. Sister's big bosom.

"WOOOOOooooooo!" T.Sister hollers as the door slams.

The church ladies help T. Sister clean off her bosom. They climb into the church outreach van and speed away.

Mother Mattie and Azalea continue to clean the kitchen. Mattie begins to hum, then slowly sings. "Hmmmmm-hmmmmmmm . . . hmm . . . me a home . . . I'm building me a home. I'm building me a home . . ."

Azalea joins her mother, "I'm building me a home."

They both sing, "Oh, my Lord. Oh, my God. What shall I do? What . . . shall . . . I . . . do?"

"Oh, your father loooved that song!" Mattie says. "I can see him now, always right up there—huh!—in the church choir singin' his heart out!"

"That's the only song Daddy knew!" Azalea says, and they both laugh.

"Your father started singing that song when we first got married," Mattie says. "He always wanted a nice, but not too large home for us. He worked real hard as an apprentice in Mason's Funeral Home. He always said, 'One day, Mattie, I'll own my own funeral home.' Huh! And he did it too. Hm hm hm . . .

"He was so proud of his funeral home and he treated the people right. He buried more people for free than anyone else in town would have. He wanted a family business for his children to continue the tradition of just treating people right, because that's all that mattered to him. If the funeral parlor across town wouldn't bury people with no money, then John came to the rescue!

"You know, John kept a clean funeral home with A+ ratings from the state. And he always kept two brand new backups of those embalming tables in the house. Child! The funerals weren't fancy, but they were decent, clean, and fair. I never understood why folks say they would rather go to Mason's Funeral Home first, but would only choose Johnson's Funeral Parlor as a second choice."

Azalea grabs her mother's hand as tears begin to fall down Mattie's face.

"We'll get through this, Momma. We've got to do what Daddy wanted us to do, as a family."

"I remember the day you were born. Your daddy delivered you right there on the spot. I went into early labor and all he had time to do was lay me down on one of those embalming tables. Child, yo daddy he was so nervous! But he did it!

"The whole time, he was humming, 'I'm building me a home.' Girl, when you came out and started screaming, woo, he looked at your brown eyes and said, 'Her eyes are brown, but they are radiant as azaleas, and that is how you got your name.

"Azalea Gwennamore Johnson. Gwen is my middle name and your daddy added *"amore"* for love. That's how you got your whole name. Azalea Gwennamore Johnson. Your entire name meant love to us. Then, the next year, I was pregnant again with your brother."

The women are silent for a moment.

"Mamma, you don't have to relive this all over again. It's OK."

"Naw, it's not OK. This time I made it to the hospital, carried the child the full nine months, and, and your baby brother didn't make it, but one day." The tears start pouring down her face even more rapidly than before.

"Oh, I wanted John to have a son, a John Junior, but I guess it was never meant to be. The doctor told me that if I tried to have any more children, it would kill me. I hated that. I told John I was willing to do it anyway! I wanted him to have a son, but John insisted I get my tubes tied, and from then on out we just tried to give you everything we didn't have."

"And everything I didn't want!" Azalea says.

"What do you mean, everything you didn't want? John worked hard for you to go to college, but instead you left home and went to New York City! You said you wanted to be an actress on Broadway! You sho' hurt your daddy when you left."

"I left because Daddy wanted me to be someone I didn't want to be. I didn't want to be in no funeral home business. That was Daddy's dream, not mine. That was Daddy's dream for John Junior.

"Besides, I got tired of the kids picking on me when I was in school. Calling me Morticia! Saying crazy things like, 'How ya living?' 'Anybody checkin' out today?' 'How's Herman and the rest of the Munsters?' And, asking crazy questions like, "Do you really know the Adams family?'

"Oh, Mamma! I just couldn't take it no more and I wanted to get away! I wanted to go to Broadway to be a successful actress, but nobody told me that I would have to play a maid, a prostitute, or a slave girl every single DARN time I got a part!"

"Watch yourself! Nobody swears in John's house!"

"I'm sorry Mamma," Azalea says, tears falling down her face, "but that's just how I felt!"

Softly, Mattie says, "Your daddy loved you more than anything else. You missed out on a wonderful man during your so-called 'grown years' of life."

"Mama, I'm 43-years-old, divorced, no children, and I came back home to help you with Daddy. I wouldn't want to be anywhere else in the world right now, Mama."

"Yeah, you didn't have a choice but to come back home. The same home you ran away from when you were 18-years-old. There were a lot of years that rolled by, but your daddy, he understood all those auditions you say you had to go to. We both understood. I missed you too," Mattie says with a wale.

"Maybe John was right when he asked the question," she begins to singing softly, "Oh, my Lord. Oh, my God. What shall I do? Oh, my Looord. Ooooh, myyyy God. What shall I do?"

Embracing, they both sing in harmony. "Ooh, my Looord. Ooooh, myyyy God. What shall I doooo?"

"Oh, that sounds so nice." Mattie smiles. "It feels good to have great memories of your daddy."

Chapter Three

Two weeks later, Mattie and Azalea are at the office of Mr. Tom Simpton, *Family Attorney.*

"Mattie," the man says as he looks at the woman. "You know, your husband was a thrifty man! He never bought fancy clothes, but—heh, heh—he did buy one suit a year. He called that his improvement on the business!"

Everyone nervously laughs and smiles.

"I'm going to miss him, Mattie. He and I never had a legal agreement, just a handshake. I'm proud to be associated with such a distinguished citizen from Dublin. Hey, John was right though! Every year he outgrew his only suit. Then, he donated it back to the funeral parlor to provide for any family who needed a suit but couldn't afford one. Ha, ha! And that was his improvement on the business! Ha! Ha!"

Mattie gives a hearty laugh and yells out, "Oh, Toooooom!"

Everyone laughs.

"But down to serious matters," Tom says as his forehead wrinkles, "John changed his will about three months before he passed away. He told me that he had changed his mind about leaving the funeral property to the neighborhood. He knew nobody would want to re-open it, since the neighborhood's value went down during his illness. He felt like folks didn't want to help folks no more. He felt if everything was done just for the money, then the price ain't worth it if you gotta be a paid friend. That's why we never signed a contract. We didn't need to."

"You know," Mattie says thoughtfully, "it was John's dream to have a family business continue at the funeral home. Tom, I don't know what I'm going to do!"

"Mama," Azalea butts in. "Calm down and let's listen to what Mr. Simpton has to say first. Remember, we said we're gonna do what Daddy wanted us to do."

Mr. Simpton calls to his secretary, a petite, light-skinned lady sitting in the room next door. "Rose, bring me the Johnson file, please."

The intercom system crackles as Rose asks, "WOULD THAT BE WALTER JOHNSON, GEORGE JOHNSON, or DR. BENJAMIN JOHNSON?"

The loud volume on the intercom causes Azalea to jump up from her seat, which startles Mr. Simpton.

"BACK SPASMS!" Azalea explains. "Back spasms. I have them sometimes."

"John Johnson," Mr. Simpton says to Rose. "Bring me the file for JOHN Johnson!"

"Is that John A. JohnSON, JOHN COLE JohnSON, John HEZEkiah JOHNSON, or is it . . . " the intercom cuts out after blaring the beginning of Rose's response.

"JUST JOHN JOHNSON!" Mr. Simpton yells.

The door flies open, and in swishes a woman who is snapping gum, and sporting a ridiculous finger wave hairstyle.

"Here you are Mr. Simpton!" Rose says as she turns and stares at Azalea. "Azalea, is that you? You haven't changed a bit. Well, you do look a little more, shall we say, 'live-li-er' since high school! Ha! Ha! Ha!"

"Oooohhhh-ooo, scary still, huh?" Azalea says. "And girl, your hair is still healthy, I see! It looks like a highway going through a mountain cliff."

Rose pats the top of her head, "Oh you like it? I do it myself!"

"You're kidding," Azalea responds sarcastically. I just knew you caught a flight to California or New York to get it done by one of those professional stylists. Oh, girl! You did that yo-SELF? You so creative!"

"Huh?" Mattie asks as she looks at Rose's hair with a stumped look on her face.

"That will be all, Rose!" Mr. Simpton says.

Rose pats her hair again and smiles as she swishes back out of Mr. Simpton's office.

"Tom," Mattie says. "Please tell us what's in the will! I can't take too much of this today. Just read the will so we can carry on my John's wishes."

"Calm down, Mama," Azalea says impatiently. "Mr. Simpton is about to do that. Right, Mr. Simpton? Go on now! READ THE WILL!"

"I, John Johnson," Mr. Simpton coughs out. "On this 18th day of May, in the year of our Lord, in 1998, in the city of Macon, in the county of Bibb, in the state of Georgia, in the country of these United States of AMER-IC-CA . . . "

"READ THE WILL!" Azalea shouts. "Oops, excuse me. Read the will, pleeease?" She says as she batts her eyes at the man.

Mr. Simpton briefly looks sideways at Azalea and then continues reading. "I hereby leave 100% of all of my personal belongings in the city of Macon, in the county of Bibb, in the state of Georgia, in the country of these United States of AMER-IC-CA, including complete ownership of our home, cars, and a personal savings of $125,000 to my one and only devoted and loving wife, Mattie Gwennamay Johnson.

"And, I leave to my one and only child, Azalea Gwennamore Johnson, whom I brought into this world on November 16, 1955, in the city of . . ."

Azalea interrupts and slams the papers in Mr. Simpton's hand down onto his desk.

"Oooh, I'm sorry! Muscle spasms. These muscle spasms! But, please, READ THE WILL!" Azalea shouts.

"I leave to you, complete ownership of the home and all of your birth possessions, including the safety deposit box with $60,000 cash," Mr. Simpton finishes.

Confused, Azalea asks, "Why does he feel he needs to leave *me* the house, if he also left Mama complete ownership of the house? Are we co-executors or something? I'm sure there's a mistake! Did your secretary get some of that hairspray on this will? Or maybe, she got the wrong Johnson file? You know she's 'Johnson dumb' and those hair chemicals be gettin' to her brain!"

Screaming through the wall, Rose shouts, "NO, I'M NOT! No, I didn't! And no, it ain't!"

Everyone jumps, shocked by Rose's voice. Mattie begins to laugh.

"Mamma! Don't laugh at her. She ain't funny! Mamma, I'm telling you!" Azalea says, but Mattie just continues to laugh. "Don't blow her head up cause she can't get nothing else under that Route Twisty-6 hairdo," Azalea continues as Mattie begins to double over with laughter.

"I don't think she's funny. MAMMA! What's so funny? Oh, so now, *now* you see that highway of a hairdo? Ha! Ha! Didn't I tell you it was ugly? Is that what you laughing about? Mamma?"

Azalea turns away from her mother and starts in on the lawyer. "Ah! Mr. Simpton, how we gonna carry out Daddy's wishes with this conflicting paperwork? Please don't be offended if I break this down for you, but something's not right here. How in the world do you leave complete ownership of a house to two people? Not that it matters to us, but for legal purposes, your office must represent clarity!"

Mattie laughs even harder.

"Mamma, are you alright?" Azalea turns back and forth between her mother and Tom. "Mr. Simpton! Do you see what this is doing to my poor mama? This is just too much pressure for her in one day."

Mattie continues to laugh.

"Mamma? Hold on, Mama. We gonna get this straightened out. Mr. Simpton, you've got to go over these things with your paralegal!" Azalea says as if she is taking control of the situation.

Mattie laughs uncontrollably then she takes a few deep breaths to regain her composure. "Hey! Hey! Hee! Hee! That John! Ha! Ha! Ha! That John! That John! That John! Ha, ha!"

"That John, huh? Old Geezer didn't know how to add percentages or what?" Azalea says. "Ha! Ha! Mama, that's what your John did! Ha! Ha! Daddy left us the same place, so we can be together! Ma, now, that's love, but didn't he know he didn't have to give me 100% of the home too? Ha! Ha! You know, I really haven't been here in so long. It feels like a new place to me anyway. So, I guess we'll be sort of like college roommates, huh? Ha-Ha! Mama?"

Mattie laughs and rolls her eyes. "Child, Don't you, hee-hee-hee, don't downplay your daddy's intelligence. He may not had an education, but he had intelligence! Hee! Hee! Ha! Ha! John knew just what he was doing!"

Puzzled, Azalea asks, "What do you mean?"

"Honey, hee-hee, your birth home! Ha-ha-ha-haaa! Your birth home is, ha, ha, hee-hee, it's the funeral parlor! Ahhh, ha, ha!" laughs Mattie.

"THE FUNERAL PARLOR?" Azalea shouts. "WHAT AM I GONNA DO WITH A FUNERAL PARLOR? I DON'T WANT NO FUNERAL PARLOR! READ THAT PAPER AGAIN, MR. SIMPTON! I DEMAND A RE-READ! RE-READ IT!"

Mr. Simpton wags his head and says, "There's one catch though."

"A CATCH? What kind of a catch?" Azalea asks as she pulls her chin back into her neck. "What is this? A fishing tournament? A baseball game for my inheritance? Well, I ain't playing! The only catchin' I'm doin' is the first flight out as soon as sunlight in the morning hits the road. CAUSE I'm out of here! I don't want no FUNERAL PARLOR!"

"Azalea!" Mattie scolds her daughter as if she were a little girl. "Stop your screaming, Child. Besides, we've got to carry out your father's wishes, remember?"

Azalea sits down, then stand back up again suddenly.

"Muscle spasms! Muscle spasms! What is the *one catch*, Mr. Simpton?"

Mr. Simpton pulls the stack of papers back up to his face and continues to read, "I leave the birth home to Azalea provided that she moves in . . ."

Azalea abruptly interrupts, "MOVES IN? MOVE IN AN OLD DELAPIDATED FUNERAL HOME? ARE YOU CRAZY?"

"Moves in," Mr. Simpton continues, "within three days . . ."

This time, Azalea completely jumps out of her chair. "THREE DAYS? ONE, PLUS ONE, PLUS ONE? THREE DAYS?"

"Three days, and immediately designs plans to bring the property values back up to a decent city code of standards that stimulates growth and positive improvements in the neighborhood. Signed, John Johnson, May 18th, 1998."

Azalea falls faint on the floor with a thud. Rose rushes into the room and begins to sprinkle ice and water droplets from her tall drink cup onto Azalea's face to revive her.

"Muscle spasms! Muscle spasms!" Azalea moans from the carpet.

Chapter Four

Back at the house, Mattie is helping Azalea take clothes out of the chest of drawers to pack them in one of Azalea's suitcases.

"Mama, why did Daddy build the funeral home an hour away in Dublin, Georgia? I thought this was supposed to be a family business? What *family business* is in another town where the family doesn't even live?"

Defiantly, Azalea begins to unpack the suitcases and put her clothes back into the chest of drawers. Mattie takes the clothes back out of the drawer and packs them back into one of Azalea's suitcases. Mother and Daughter repeat this routine during the entire conversation.

"Honey," Mattie starts, "your daddy made sure we had two homes. One in Macon, and one in Dublin. Right now, we've just . . ."

"Got to follow through with all of his wishes!" Azalea chimes in and says in unison with her mother as they finish the sentence.

Suddenly, there is a knock at the front screen door of their home.

"Now, who would that be?" Mattie stops packing Azalea's luggage and heads toward the front door.

Plopping down on her bed, Azalea looks on her dresser and stares at a childhood picture of her hanging on her daddy's shoulders. She shakes her head from left to right as she continues to stare at the picture. Her eyes move to stare at her own reflection in the mirror hanging above the chest of drawers. She reflects for a moment, and then stands up and pulls the clothes out of the chest of drawers and throws them quickly into her opened suitcase.

"Oh, allll-right! I'll go!" Azalea murmurs while looking at her reflection and staring at the picture.

Meanwhile, Mattie answers the front door. "Yes, may I help you?"

A handsome police officer is standing on the other side of the front porch screen door. "Howdy, Mrs. Johnson. I'm Officer Terry with the Macon Police Department and I have a few questions that I'd like to ask you."

"Listen now, Officer, I don't know nothing 'bout that moonshine yall found on the property five years ago. I already told the police . . ."

"Uh, no, Ma'am. This ain't about that, Mrs. Johnson. We've closed that case. I need to ask you a few things about your husband's funeral procession."

"What about the funeral procession?"

"Did you notice anything strange as your procession crossed over Jeffersonville Highway?"

"No, Officer, I didn't," Mattie says slowly, trying to remember. "I couldn't see anything other than visions of my husband and me. I was thinking to myself, 'Oh, this is it! God gave us a good life together and now, now my John is gone!' I'm sorry, Officer. You didn't come to hear all of this, did you? Won't you come in and have some good cold iced tea?"

"It's OK, Mrs. Johnson. I understand and I'm very sorry about your loss. Well, thank you for your time. I'll take a rain check on the tea, and I'm sorry to have bothered you. Mr. Johnson was as good as a citizen could be. He was a decent man in this community."

"Yall check on me from time to time," Mattie said, "and make sure this old lady is alright, you hear?"

"Yes, Ma'am," Officer Terry says.

Overhearing the conversation from her room, Azalea says, "I saw something."

"What?" Mattie asks her daughter.

"I thought this white van was gonna run right smack into us at the Jeffersonville intersection."

As he pulls out a small notebook and a pen, Officer Terry asks, "Can you tell me how many people you saw in the van?"

"What white van?" Mattie asks, a bit confused.

"I saw two people in a white speeding van!" Azalea exclaimed. "It looked like there was someone else riding in the back, but I'm not sure. But I know that I saw two people with hard hats on in the front seats. They were definitely in a white van!"

"Azalea!" Mattie said, "I didn't know."

"Are you sure Miss?" the Officer asks.

"Heck yeah, I'm sure! You don't usually forget the moment when your life just flashes in front of your eyes! That was definitely a crazy lunatic driving that white van. I'll never forget it! Not to mention, there was some stupid cop chasing them, which almost caused them to hit us! How could I forget a moment like that?"

Officer Terry dropped his eyes slightly and said, "I guess I won't forget it either, especially since I'm that stupid cop that was chasing them! Well, I was actually the officer in pursuit of the van. I apologize, but I have to ask you if you saw which direction they went after barging though your father's funeral procession?"

"Yeah," Azalea said, "they hit the Jeffersonville Highway and then they hauled a--. . ."

"Azalea Gwennamore Johnson! Bite your tongue!" Mattie interrupts.

"Hauled *poke* down US 80, shall we say it that way?" Azalea says snippily.

"Azalea Johnson?" Officer Terry asked with surprise in his voice. "Didn't you used to be in the drama club at Westside High School?"

"Yes, I did, but that was over 20 something years ago. Who are you?"

"It's me, Terry. Terry Johnson."

"Terry Johnson?" Azalea asks, "The fat kid that had to play the part of a boulder in the play *Crater Creations of Earth*? Terry Johnson, the only other kid besides me that everybody picked on?

Remember, they said you and me were Johnson and Johnson—the oddballs!"

"Yeah, they did," Officer Terry laughs remembering, "but we always said . . ."

Azalea chimes in and they both say, "Same last name, but different families!"

"Who are your folks, son?" Mattie asks.

"Dr. Benjamin Johnson was my father. He died seven years ago. I guess it doesn't matter how decent your parent's occupation is, kids can be cruel." Turning to Azalea, he says, "Thank you very much for the information, Azalea. I may need to follow up later with more questions. I hope that's OK?"

"What did those folks do?" Mattie asks. "The folks in the white van. What did they do?"

Officer Terry pauses, then turns to head toward his patrol car. "They stole a million dollars from a widow in Chicago," he says.

As the cop climbs into his patrol car and drives away, Azalea throws her arms around her mother and escorts her back into the house.

"Why don't you go out, unwind, and have yourself a good time, Azalea?" Mattie says. "You can't stay up under me all the time. I'll be all right. Go out and enjoy yourself tonight. It's your last night in town."

"I was thinking about going to the O.S. Club. They've got a live band and some of the best chicken wings in Macon. Not to mention good drinks and single men!"

Both women laugh.

"Sounds like a place that I may have to visit soon, huh?" Mattie says.

Azalea laughs. "Mamma, I can't believe you just said that!"

"Go ahead, Honey. You need some time to be by yourself to think about what you're gonna do with the funeral parlor. Besides, I think I need some time alone to think about things for me to do too. Taking care of your daddy was my life, and taking care of me was his life. Now, I've got to learn to take care of myself."

The women stand silently for a moment.

"Thank you, Mama. I'll go and get changed, and maybe I will hit the town. Maybe I'll call up Samantha," Azalea says hesitantly. "You know, she says that I was her only friend. Maybe that was because back then nobody else would give her the time of day. Ooh, Mama, they use to say she was so ugly that she'd scare a ghost!"

The women laugh again.

"I love you, Mama. And I loved my daddy. I just wish I could've . . ."

Mattie interrupts her daughter, "You just didn't understand him, Honey. You just didn't understand him. Now you go on, get yourself looking good, and get yourself ready to go have a good time tonight!"

Tears drop from Azalea's face. Mattie smiles, throws her arms around her daughter, and starts humming *I'm Building Me a Home*.

A few minutes later, Azalea is on the phone. "Samantha, this is Azalea. Azalea Johnson."

"Azalea Johnson?" Samantha asks. "It's been a long time since I heard from my best friend! Hey, I'm sorry about your father."

"Thank you for your prayers," Azalea says. "Tonight, I want to just go out and relax a bit. Do they still have a good time at the O.S. Club?"

"Girl, tonight is *The Impromptu Jam Session* with DC, Our Biggest Fan from WIBB Radio, and his special guest tonight is the *MVP Band!*"

"You mean DC's gonna to be there live tonight?" Azalea squeals. "He's the biggest radio star in Central Georgia!"

"Yeah, and I've been practicing his weekly sing-a-long song, *Stand By Me*, in case he calls me onstage to sing with him and the MVP Band!"

"Girl, let's do it! Let's go out with the grown folks at the O.S. Club. I'll meet you there!"

"It'll be like old times like when we used to go to the talent shows back in high school!" Samantha says.

Both scream with excitement, hang up the phone and begin to get dressed for the party.

Chapter Five

In front of the command center at the police station, the Police Chief begins a brief meeting with Officers Johnson, Brandon and Handley.

"Alright everybody, I need an update on the white van!" The Chief begins. "Officer Johnson has confirmation that are at least two suspects, and possibly one more unidentified passenger who was riding in the back of the van. We have the tag number: DAK369L. The van was last seen traveling east on Jeffersonville Highway, headed toward Highway 80. Alright, let's be observant, go out there, and find them. I want those criminals off these roads and behind bars!"

The officers say, "Yes, sir!" and move along to begin their duties. As he uploads his report, Officer Johnson murmurs, "I've got to find these people."

"Johnson," Officer Brandon calls out. "You about to get three days off in a row? Must be nice."

"Yeah, I can't wait until tomorrow," Johnson replies, "I guess I'll take my lady out to dinner."

"You still seein' the same lady?" Officer Handley butts in.

"Well, kind-of. She's not really my type, but she is a nice girl," Johnson says.

"Nice enough to spend the night, huh? You little sneaky son-of-a-gun! You like to rescue the damsel in distress and then collect your rewards. Ha, Ha, ha," Brandon mocks.

"Cut it out, Brandon, you know I'm not like you!" Johnson says as he turns his back and continues his work.

"Suuuurrrrreee," Handley laughs.

Johnson shakes his head, smiles, and says, "Get out of here!"

Chapter Six

As Azalea waits for Samantha at the front door of the O.S. Club, a toothless guy approaches her and reaches out for her arm.

"Say, Baby," the creepy guy says, "I'd like to put some ketchup on yo' fries."

Snatching her arm away and kneeing him in the groin, Azalea blusters, "What about some hot sauce on your nuggets instead?"

Another guy approaches. "Hey, Baby. You look like the girl in my dreams."

"No, that wasn't me," Azalea quipped. "That was my sister. We look just alike. She told me about you. You were the man who got his hand chopped off by a crazy woman standing in front of a club."

The man takes a step back and shakes his head. "Lunatic!" He mutters.

As the man walks away, Samantha arrives. She is wearing a very bright, 1970s, psychedelic type of outfit.

"Azalea!" Samantha yells.

"Samantha!"

The girls hug and Samantha leads the way to the front door. "Come on, Girl. Let's get inside of this club before DC hits the stage. He is **so** fine, and I'm so nervous! I really believe he is going to ask me to sing tonight! Any good men passed by yet?"

"Girl, you should've seen the bums I met while I was waiting on you. I didn't know whether to call security or a priest!" Azalea says.

As they walk into the club, The MVP Band is on stage and the lead singer, Ms. San starts singing Betty Wright's song *Tonight Is The Night*.

"What are you drinking, Girl?" Samantha asks. "I'll go to the bar and pick up our drinks while you get us a seat!"

"Just water. Water and lemon," Azalea says.

"Water and lemon? You've got to be kidding me. It's your last night out for a while so you know we've got to celebrate! Huh? Water and lemon?"

"Look, you won't get me with that peer pressure jazz. I'm too old for that, and you know your old self is too old to think about peers or peer pressure," Azalea says as they both laugh.

"Girl, you know your peers are George Washington, Ben Franklin, and Miss Jane Pittman," Samantha says with a grin.

"Miss Jane Pittman! Now don't try to convince me into sipping one of those strong Long Island Iced Teas. You're . . ."

Samantha cuts her off, "Aazzaaalea!" The girls continue to laugh.

"OK, OK, OK, OK!" Azalea gives in. "Tell Annette to fix me one! You calling me Miss Jane Pittman! Girl, you were friends with Miss Jane Pittman's mama!"

They continue to laugh as Samantha goes to the bar to pick up the drinks. Azalea begins to pull out a chair from any empty table as a familiar figure reaches for the other available chair at the same table.

"Azalea?" the woman asks.

"Rose?"

"I'm surprised to see you here!" Rose says, smacking her gum.

"Well, I came out with my friend, Samantha. You know Samantha, don't you?"

"Oh, yeah. Is she still as ugly as she used to be? You know what they say, time waits for no one."

Fed up, Azalea snaps, "She happens to be my best friend, and I don't think you should go around picking on people all the time. You're just as old as the rest of us, and what you're saying is just not nice. Anyway, have you looked at yourself in the mirror lately because your hair is on fire!"

Touching her hair as though she's been complimented, Rose shyly says, "Oh, thank you, Azalea. You don't look too bad yourself, except you could change your . . ."

"Ladies?" a male voice interrupts.

"Hello, Officer Johnson. We meet again," Azalea blushes. "Rose, this is Officer Johnson. Officer Johnson, this is Rose."

Johnson and Rose smile as Azalea introduces them to each other.

"I know him, Azalea," Rose says with a laugh. "He's my date!" Turning to Johnson, she says, "Um, Terry, I thought this would be our table, but I guess we'll have to find one closer to the stage. I want to make sure that I'm close enough for DC to see me so that he can call me up to sing with him."

"You and everybody else," Terry says.

Azalea's mouth drops open as Rose grabs Terry's hand and walk away just as Samantha returns with two very colorful Long Island Iced Teas.

"Girl, let's party!" Samantha says, oblivious to what just happened.

"Yeah, let's party," Azalea says nonchalantly.

The lead singer of the MVP Band, Ms. San, which is short for Sandra, begins to introduce DC.

"We going to call up Macon's worldwide radio man—all the way from WIBB and V102. It's the legendary DC, Your Biggest Fan!" Sandra shouts out.

DC enters the stage, dressed in one of his finest suit as fans pat him on the back and snap pictures.

"What's up, Macon?" DC smiles. "Give it up for the MVP Band!"

The enthusiastic crowd shouts back in response.

"First of all, let's put our hands together for everybody spending green money in a black-owned business!" The audience claps wildly. "This is the truest sense of supporting black-owned business! We got black folks and white folks and all races here tonight!" The crowd continues to yell. "This is the part of the show we call the Impromptu Jam Session where we give you the chance to sing with the band. Is that alright with you?"

The crowd hollers, "Yes!"

"Now this is what I'm going to do," DC explains. "I'm gonna split the club up into two parts, right down the middle. The side on my right will be side one, and the side on my left will be side two."

Azalea is on side two and Rose is on side one. Rose immediately makes attempts to get the folks on side one to start yelling and making the loudest noise, to get DC's attention.

"DC, DC! Over here!" Rose shouts.

"Alright side one. You know how we do it! Are you ready?" DC asks.

The crowd screams, "YES!"

"Are you ready?" DC asks again.

"YES!" the crowd continues to scream even louder.

"Are you ready?" DC shouts.

"YES!"

"Say Band!" DC commands.

"BAND!"

"Say Band!"

"BAND!"

"SAY BAND!" DC gets louder.

"BAND!"

"ONE TIME!" DC changes it up.

"ONE TIME!" the crowd responds in unison.

DC throws back his arm in a James Brown type of move, and the music stops on the one beat. The drums boom as Rose jumps up and down in front of side one, cheering them on to make more noise. At the same time, Azalea appoints herself as the team leader of side two.

"Oh, side two, it looks like you've got work to do, because side one is off the hook!" DC shouts. "Side two, are you ready?"

"YES!" Side two screams.

"ARE YOU READY!" DC shouts.

"YES!"

"ARE YOU READY?"

"YES!" the crowd yells.

"SAY BAND!"

"BAND!"

"SAY BAND!"

"BAND!"

"SAY BAND!"

Azalea suddenly jumps onto the stage and begins to direct side two.

"Band-sopranos, band-altos, band-tenors, band-bass!" Azalea shouts.

DC looks confused, but he blurts out his final words anyway, "TWO TIMES!"

Azalea directs side two. "TWO, TWO, TWO, TWO, TWO, TWO, TWO, TWO, TWO, TWOOOOOO!"

DC throws his hand in the air and the band stops the music on the second beat. BOOM BOOM! The drums go off as the crowd erupts in applause.

"Well, I've got to tell you," DC says, "Side two won tonight! Give it up for them! Alright, bartenders, side two gets one drink on the house! A tall glass of water—heavy on the ice!"

BOOM! BOOM! The drums go off again.

Rose is fuming as waitresses rush to side two to take orders for free drinks.

DC begins to sing *Stand By Me* as he walks through the audience looking for eager and willing participants to sing a part of the verses with him. "When the night has come, and the land is dark . . ."

At the table, Samantha turns to Azalea. "Girl, you've still got it!"

Azalea, tipsy from the Long Island Iced Tea, says, "That was sooooo much fun!"

"Can I take your orders?" A waitress asks.

"Two more of those Lost Island of Gilligans!" Azalea giggles.

"Are you sure?" Samantha asks.

"Remember, I'm friends with the original Presidents. Don't forget that!" Azalea snaps. "Put peer pressure on me . . ." Giggling as she slurps down another drink, Azalea tries to speak, but her speech slurs. "Excuse me, Samantha, but I've got to go to the ladies room."

As Azalea walks away, a good looking guy walks up and begins to talk to Samantha. "Take your time, Honey," Samantha shouts to Azalea. "Take your time!"

In the restroom, as Azalea looks in the mirror she notices Rose coming out of a stall. Rose stands in front of the other side of the mirror and begins to powder her face. Neither woman speaks to the other.

Looking directly into the mirror at Rose's reflection, Azalea calmly says, "You know, we really don't have to relive the past. Rose, we're adults now and whether you realize it or not, we're both old enough to be grandmothers."

Looking at Azalea's reflection, Rose shrieks appalled at the idea of being a grandmother, and shoots one hand up to cover her heart.

"No need to pretend. We all know there's some gray tint under that red dye in your hair," Azalea says.

"Speak for yourself," Rose says. "This isn't red; it's bright auburn!"

Azalea shakes her head. "Let's just call a truce and move on with our lives. There's so much more we can do than try to tear each other a part."

Rose sighs as she drops her lipstick into the sink.

"Allow me," Azalea says as she picks up the lipstick.

"OK. Truce," Rose says as she stares at Azalea.

"Truce," Azalea says as she rolls out the lipstick and starts putting it on Rose's lips.

"Girl, you looking good now!" Azalea exclaims. "C'mon, let's go back out there and jam with DC and the MVP Band."

"It's time to party!" Rose screams with excitement.

Azalea walks out first, and Rose follows. As they walk through the crowd, people begin to stare and laugh.

"Don't let them worry you, Azalea," Rose says. "You're not Morticia anymore!"

"I know that's right, Girl!" Azalea chuckles.

"Find someone else to pick on!" Rose says as she passes the crowd. "You just look forward and keep your head up, Azalea. "But maybe you should've worn a nicer dress . . ."

"Maybe so," Azalea laughs.

Rose finds her seat next to Officer Johnson. He looks astonished as she sits down.

"Baby, what did you do to yourself?" He demands to know.

"I just freshened up," replies Rose as she smiles like a beauty queen.

Meanwhile, back at Azalea's table, Samantha is talking to two gorgeous men.

"This is Marcus, and this is Edwin," Samantha introduces them to Azalea.

"Girl, I hate to ruin the party, but I've really got to go and get some rest for the drive to Dublin tomorrow," Azalea says, uninterested in the men.

"Oh, Azalea! Not yet! We just got some new faces to sit with us. Did I say *handsome* new faces?"

"Did you say Dublin?" Marcus asks Azalea. "I live in Dublin."

"Really? You don't act like the typical person from Dublin, Georgia. Especially with that accent!" Azalea says.

"Let's just say, my job transferred me there," Marcus replies.

"Well, I've been, kind of, transferred there too!" Azalea laughs.

"Hopefully, you'll give me a chance to take you to dinner at some point?" Marcus asks.

"Certainly. I'd love to see you again, but I've got a long day tomorrow and I've got to go. Samantha, am I leaving without you, or are we going to leave together?"

"We didn't come together, so I guess we ain't got to leave together," Samantha laughs. "Girl, I'll come see you after you move to Dublin. Bye, Girl!" Turning back to the guys Samantha says, "Now, where were we, Mr. Edwin?"

"Azalea, hey, I'll walk you to your car," Marcus says.

"Thanks. I'd like that since *my best friend* has abandoned me," Azalea says. Azalea and Marcus exit the O.S. Club and head for the parking lot.

Back on the inside, Officer Johnson is still sitting at the VIP table. Rose is so drunk she is dancing ridiculously in front of Officer Johnson's seat.

"Rose, where is your mirror?" Johnson asks.

"My *mirror*? My mirror for what, Terry?"

"Just give me your mirror!"

"OK," Rose says as she digs around in her purse. "Here is my mirror. You know a *beautiful* woman *always* keeps a mirror!"

"Give it to me!" Terry says.

"Well, OK, *but be careful,* Terry! My picture is inserted on one side. What are you going to do with a mirror?"

Terry holds the mirror up for Rose, and she begins to smile as she peeks at herself. The smile turns quickly into a frown when she suddenly realizes her lipstick has been put on in a zigzag manner.

"Aaaaaawwwwww!" Rose screams, then faints.

Chapter Seven

The next morning, Azalea loads the car with luggage, hot plates, cleaning utensils, and a baseball bat—just in case. She finishes packing and heads to the front porch to say good-bye to her mother. "Now, you do what your father intended you to do," Mattie says.

"What? Have a heart attack?" Azalea smirks.

"Girl, you know better than that. Your father only wanted the best for his baby girl."

"Well, why does he want me to go live in a FUNERAL PARLOR for THREE DAYS? Ain't no way you can say that's his best for me. Maybe he did want to name me Morticia! That's the only woman I can think of who would be happy to move into a funeral parlor, period! But I'm Azalea, and I don't want to spend three days, one day, or even 15 minutes in a funeral parlor!"

By this time, her mother had tears in her eyes from laughing. "I'm sure gonna miss you Azalea."

"I'm gonna miss you too, Mama, but I'm a big girl and I can handle this by myself. Besides, Dublin ain't but an hour away from here." She shakes her head a little as tears begin to slide down her face. "I got to go now, Mama. I'll call you when I get there!"

Azalea walks to the car, climbs in and begins buckling her seatbelt.

"Do you have your new cellica-phone?" Mattie yells at Azalea.

"Yeah, Ma. I LOVE YOU! BYEEEEE!" Azalea yells out the window as she cranks the car.

"Bye, Baby. Call me!" Mattie yells as Azalea speeds off down the road.

About twenty minutes into her trip, Azalea is singing a song by Gladys Knight and the Pips that's playing on the radio.

"Got-to-make-the-best of, best-of, best-of . . . a-bad-situa-tion, si-tua-tion. Woo-oo-oo-oo-oo-oo, Woo-oo-oo-oo-oo-oo, Woo-oo-oo-oo-oo-oo!"

A police siren begins to sound.

WOOOOOOOOOOOOOOOOOOOOOAAAAAAAAAAAAH HHHHWIP-WIP.

"Woo-oo-oo-o-oh-oh-hohoh. . . Holy-snap!" Azalea says to herself as she pulls over to the side of the road. "I'm on my way to live in a funeral home and I get a speeding ticket on the way there? No way! I ain't in no hurry to get to the funeral home, so how in the world am I getting a ticket? I can't believe it!"

Azalea looks straight ahead and holds her hands out of the window as the police officer approaches the driver's side of her car.

"You can put your hands back in the car. This is Macon, Georgia," the officer says.

"I'm sorry, but that's what's required in other cities," Azalea says as she continues to hold her hands outside of the window, all the while she keeps her view straight out the windshield, totally avoiding eye-contact with the officer.

"May I see your license and insurance card please?" The officer asks.

Still looking straight ahead, Azalea reaches into her pocketbook with one hand, pull outs her information, and gives the paperwork to the officer. She has yet to look at him.

"I didn't know you weighed . . . a hundred and . . ." the officer begins.

Azalea's mouth drops wide open in surprise and offense. She abruptly turns her head around to look at the man, and her face softens.

"Officer Terry Johnson!" Azalea interrupts him. "Am I glad to see you, I think," she adds.

"Let's see. The last time I *saw you,* was, I believe you had signed your handiwork on my date at a certain nightspot. Hum. The O.S. Club, remember?"

"About that . . . Hey, let me explain . . ."

"Don't mention it," Officer Terry laughs. "I couldn't have thought of a better prank myself!"

Azalea laughs. "Well, you got to give a girl credit . . ."

"No, I got to give a girl a ticket! You were going 75 in a 55 mile per hour zone. The radar picked you up at two different overpasses and they called your tag number in on all bulletins."

"What? Are you serious? Was I going that fast? Come on! It's not like I'm the first person to go over the speed limit in this town!"

"Of course, you're not. We've got a feeling those sneaky thieves may stake out in this area, so we're checking any suspicious or speeding vehicles. I guess you check out this time, but you do need to slow down. Dublin ain't going nowhere." Officer Johnson hands Azalea's paperwork back to her and puts his ticket book into his pocket.

"You're right about that. Thanks Officer Johnson."

"Hey, it's Terry! You've always known me by my first name so keep calling me Terry. Cool?"

Azalea smiles, shakes her head, and drives away.

Chapter Eight

Azalea talks to herself as she dusts the kitchen area of her new home. The small house sits on the front part of the land where the funeral parlor is located.

"All of this for $60,000? $60,000 in a safety deposit box? A safety deposit box, huh? The safety deposit box! Where in the world is that safety deposit box?"

Azalea picks up her cell phone and speed dials her mother. "Ma, I forgot to ask you, where did daddy keep the safety deposit box?"

"You know, I never knew. Your daddy always said he had one, but I never knew where it was. He always thought that I would spend everything. I guess he was right to hide the money from me, but, anyway. I've never seen the safety deposit box."

"OK, so maybe there isn't one, huh, Ma? So, OK. Ma, I'm packing up now and coming home."

"But you just got there! Now your daddy didn't lie. Well, except to nosey Ms. Henny, but he wouldn't lie about *this,* so you stay there and do what you're supposed to do and you will find the safety deposit box."

"Thanks, Ma. Bye now," Azalea hangs up and begins to talk to herself as she stares at the ceiling. "OK. I'm going to walk through this house to see what's in every room and I'm not going to be scared. Now, OK, this is the li-iiv-ing room for li-iiving people to sit and talk, so, *dead people,* don't talk to me … Yall stay in the *back of the house,* and I'll stay in the front. OK?"

Azalea looks up and down the walls as she walks through the hallway into the next room.

"So, this is the *bathroom* and this room is only for me and my guests, so I'd appreciate it if *yall* don't be standing behind me in the mirror when I'm in the bathroom. You know what I'm saying? I'm already regular! So, you know what I mean? Any other surprises may make me thinner than a retouch!"

All of a sudden Azalea hears a sound coming from the front door. Knock. Knock. Knock. Knock. Knock. Knock!

"Aaaaww-AAA-aaaa-Ahhhhh!" screams Azalea as she spins around.

Knock, knock, knock!

"Who is it?" Azalea nervously whispers.

KNOCK! KNOCK! KNOCK!

"Who-the-world-is-it?" Azalea quickly chokes out in a whisper.

"It's me! Samantha. Girl, is that you?" Samantha whispers back. "Why are we whispering? And open the door, please!"

Azalea opens the door and screams, "Samantha!"

"Azalea!" Samantha screams back. The girls hug, both seemingly in a state of relief.

"I can't believe this! You are the last person that I expected to see," Azalea says. "What are you doing here so soon? But I'm so glad to see you!"

"Girl, you know that I couldn't let you come out here and clean up this, ah, *home* by yourself. Besides, Mr. Edwin says he lives in Dublin too. We're supposed to meet at a restaurant this weekend! Ah! Azalea, this place ain't so creepy. We'll have this baby looking like a home in no time! Remember in college when we were roommates? They always said that we had the cleanest rooms because both of us believed in wiping everything down with alcohol and bleach."

Samantha comes into the house, sets down her bags, and picks up a sopping wet cleaning rag from the bucket Azalea was using. As she begins to clean the windows, she glances through the glass at the shed in the back of the house.

"Hey, I didn't know that your Dad kept a shed back there. What's out there, dead bodies or something?"

Wiping the dust from the furniture in the room, Azalea answers. "Yeah. That's the shed where my dad built most of our furniture, and most of the caskets he sold cheap to so many families in Dublin. Me and Dad spent a lot of nights working on caskets to make sure that these people had decent burials. I wasn't allowed in the other room—where he kept the bodies."

Samantha begins to clean the corner of a dusty window. As she moves the rag back and forth, an image of a Chinese woman seems to appear through the dirt and grime.

"Aaaaah-aaaahh-aaaaah!" Samantha screams.

"Aaaaaaah-aaaah-aaaaah!" Screams the Chinese lady.

Samantha looks up at the ceiling and continues screaming. "This is not happening to me!" She begins quoting the only scripture she can remember. "Yea, though I walk through the shadow of death, I will fear no evil, for this . . . is . . . my . . . ah! My country, land that I love . . . tis of thee . . . forever . . . Amen!"

The Chinese lady's mouth is moving, but her words are muted by the thick window.

"Oh, my, God! Ain't no words coming out your mouth! Azalea! Come here girl! I'm seeing things! I just saw a Chinese woman, and she ain't got no voice. She's staring at me through this window. Azalea! Answer me! Azalea! Girl, you hear me?"

Samantha looks back at the window, but the image of the woman is gone.

"AZ-AL-EA!" Samantha screams.

Samantha runs into the next room, where Azalea is supposed to be cleaning. She sees Azalea standing at the front door talking to a small Chinese lady.

"Oh, my GOD! She got to you! OOOOHH, AZALEA!" Samantha begins to cry.

"Samantha, GET-A-GRIP! This is my neighbor, Ms. Soon Lee. She brought us something to eat!"

"Hello. Please-meet-you," Ms. Soon Lee says to Samantha in broken English, strung together so fast the girls can barely understand her. "I-no-come-here-long-time. You father great man. So kind to poor people. Always bury, even when no money. Dat Mr. John-son, he missed!"

"Thank you, Ms. Soon Lee," Azalea says.

Confused, Samantha stops crying and stares at Ms. Soon Lee.

"Did you just say somethin'?" Samantha asked Ms. Soon Lee. "And what kind of accent was that? That ain't from London what I just heard, was it?"

"Ha, ha, ha! Sorry. No mean scare you. I find front door!"

"You did talk!" Samantha said. "Azalea, girl, you know I love you, but I'm needing to get the heck out of here right now! With a quickness!"

With an apologetic tone, Azalea says, "Pardon her, Ms. Soon Lee. She's been under a lot of stress. You know, man problems, menopause, and she's sweating!"

Ms. Soon Lee begins to laugh. "You need stud, huh? I see if I have spare one or two." Ms. Soon Lee then bows her head and backs out of the front door in a submissive Oriental sort of way.

Azalea and Samantha stare at each other, burst into laughter, and go back to their house cleaning.

~ Change of Scene ~

Around seven the next morning there was another sound at the front door.

THUMP! KNOCK. KNOCK. KNOCK. THUMP!

"What in the world? Do people around here sleep, or respect others who choose to sleep?" Azalea says to herself as she jumps up and begins to move the furniture she used to barricade the front door the night before.

She finally gets the doorway cleared, and opens the door. Staring straight ahead, Azalea doesn't see anyone.

"Ma'am," a small voice says. Azalea drops her eyes lower and sees a young boy standing directly in front of her. "I'm sorry, but I must misinform you that your Sunday newspaper service will be discontented, discontinity, discontin-new . . ." the boy struggles to get his words out.

"Discontinued?" Azalea asks as she looks down at the child.

"Yes, ma'am. Discontin-uwed if I don't receive your past due payment today."

"Well, how much do I owe as of today?"

"Fourteen dollars and thirty nine cents."

"OK. How about I pay you the fourteen dollars and thirty nine cents for the past due amount, plus I pay you an additional fourteen dollars and thirty nine cents to get paid up in advance for the next month's papers?"

"Gee, thanks, ma'am," the little kid says with a smile.

Azalea smiles, grabs her purse and pulls out some cash. She pays the boy and closes the door as the child hops on his bike and rides away.

SNOOORRE. The noise is coming from Samantha, who is sleeping on the couch in the living room.

Azalea walks over to the corner of the room, grabs a trashcan and a broom, and smashes them together.

WHAM!

"AAAAHHH!" Samantha screams as she jumps up and forms a cross with her fingers to ward off any ghosts.

"Girl, you need to stop rubbing those boney fingers together before this house catch on fire!" Azalea says with a laugh.

"Very funny, Azalea. I'm glad you woke me up. I've got to meet Mr. Edwin for lunch today."

"Well, thanks for coming yesterday. You are truly a friend. I guess I'll get busy and clean the rest of the house before Mama shows up for some kind of surprise inspection."

"I'll be back tomorrow to check on you. I'll bring Mr. Edwin with me. We need a strong man to turn on the hot water pump and help us move some of this heavy stuff, you know. Don't forget, you need to get hot water out here fast! My favorite aunt lives in Dublin, so you know you're always welcome to go to her place to freshen up if you need to."

"Thanks, Samantha. You've done more than enough by just being here with me. The hot water pump will be on tomorrow by mid-day. I'll take care of everything else. I probably need to do the rest of the sorting through stuff by myself anyway. It gives me a chance to get to know my father, if you know what I mean?"

"That's fine if that's what you want to do. Just don't reintroduce your father to me or nothing like that. OK?"

Samantha nervously looks up and down and around the room, just in case Mr. Johnson's ghost was hovering nearby. "Ooh, is that my cell phone ringing?"

"I don't hear nothing, Girl," Azalea said puzzled. "You ain't got no cell phone!"

"Yes, I do! I don't? Oh, I left in the car. Uh-oh, so I know it's time for me to go! I'll see YALL! I mean, you! I'll see *you* later. Bye now!"

Samantha slips on her shoes, grabs her bag, and walks briskly out the front door.

Chapter Nine

RING! RING! RING!

"Hello," Azalea says as she answers the phone.

"Hi, Azalea. This is Marcus. Remember me? I met you at the O.S. Club in Macon. I remember you said you would be in Dublin, so I wanted to know if you would be interested in having dinner with me tonight? I know you've got a lot to do, so I thought I'd call you early and give you an entire day to think about it before you turn me down."

"Marcus?" Azalea asks as she holds the phone away from her face to compose herself. "Well, I'd love to go to dinner with you, but I've got a whole lot more to do, and I really hate the thought of cleaning that shed in the back of my father's . . . my . . . ah . . . house . . . home . . . BUT, I'm sure the shed can wait till the end of the week, so what time should I be ready?"

"What about 7:30 tonight? How's that?"

"Perfect! I mean, that's fine with me because I'll be at a good stopping point by then."

"Great, what are you in the mood for? Home cooked meal or seafood?"

"Funny, Marcus. This is Dublin. There are only a few choices!"

"I tell you what, why don't you dress however you feel, and you decide what you want to eat, and I'll meet you there, but the bottom line is it must be whatever your heart desires."

"Oh, Marcus! I thought it was the other way around? Feed the man and he'll stay for life . . ."

"Maybe so, but there's not one feast worthy of your presence, my princess."

"OK, Marcus. I already said yes to dinner, but it sounds like you're working mighty hard on desert! Ha! Ha!"

"I'll see you at 7:30. Bye," Marcus says with a mischievous tone.

"Good—ah—bye. I mean, see you in a few hours?" Azalea disconnects the call, holds the phone to her chest and begins to speak to herself. "OK, I've got two hours. I need to run to the Dublin Mall and get something to wear. Oh, my goodness! I need to take a shower and I've got no hot water!"

KNOCK! KNOCK! KNOCK!

Startled, Azalea yells at the door, "WHO IS IT?"

"Hello, der! You want put food in tummy now? I bring favoritee dishee, shrimp-fry-rye wit a touch of blarney! You no starve!" Ms. Soon Lee says.

"Oh, thank you, Ms. Soon Lee. Please, pardon my rudeness, but I've got a dinner date tonight and I hope you won't be offended if I put your delicious dish in the refrigerator until tomorrow?"

"You no have re-frig-er-a-tor! You no know?"

"Oh, you are so right, Ms. Soon Lee, but I've got a cooler with ice and I'll put it there until the morning and eat it for breakfast. How's that?"

"OK. Why you no bring foodie back to my re-frig-er-a-tor? And you take hot bath, so you can feel goodie tonight, huh?"

"Oh, thank you, Ms. Soon Lee! I appreciate that. I'll be over in a few minutes. Thank you so much!"

"No worry. Does he have friend, for me? Ha! Ha!" the old woman laughs.

"Ms. Soon Lee!"

They both laugh and Azalea starts grabbing a few things to take with her. Ms. Soon Lee walks away.

"Why you no install se-cur-ity light in par-lor? You use flashy-light at night?"

"What are you talking about? I haven't been in the shed yet."

"Oh, wel-me eye-site es-like-me-hormones. On-fire dear! Ha! Ha!"

The women laugh.

Chapter Ten

Later that evening, Azalea and Marcus meet in the downtown square for a walk.

"OK, Azalea, where would my queen like to dine tonight?"

"Oh, so now I'm an older woman!"

"What do you mean, Azalea?"

"Well, earlier I was a princess. Now you say I'm a queen!"

They both laugh.

"Either way, you're royalty to me tonight," Marcus says as he bows. What do you feel like eating?"

Azalea smiles embarrassedly. "Let's flip for it. Heads, we go to Red Lobster for crab legs. Tails, we go to Red Lobster for shrimp! Ha!"

"Ok, so you want Red Lobster. I know, here's another great idea, why don't we go to Red Lobster? Ha, Ha!"

"You're funny, Marcus."

"No, you're funny, Azalea."

As they both laugh, Marcus reaches out and puts his arms around Azalea.

"Wow! I didn't realize how much I missed having a hug. This is nice."

"Sure is. Are you ready to go now?"

"Hey, perhaps a little desert don't sound too bad after all. Um, Marcus, thank you for thinking about me. I'm ready to go if you're ready."

They drive across town, arrive at the restaurant and park. A hostess greets them as they walk through the doors.

"Welcome to Red Lobster," the smiling young girl says as she stares at the two of them. "How many in your party?"

"Just me and him. Just the two of us," Azalea says as she holds up two fingers.

"Yes, just two. Thank you."

"Maybe she thought we had more folks on the way . . ."

"I wasn't sure if Casper was standing there with you, Morticia!" The hostess snapped. "My mama already schooled me on the dozens."

"What? The dozens? What you talkin' about *schooled on the dozens*, huh?" Azalea asked.

"Rose. Rose Pedolls. Rose Pedolls is my mom."

"OK. So, that explains everything. Now I understand. So I guess your elevator doesn't go to the top-floor either?"

"I'm a student at Oconee Fall Line Tech," the teenager said, flipping her hair out of her eyes and flashing her long, hot-pink-painted nails. "I'm taking up radiology. Two more years to go. What did *you* do?"

Sensing the tension, Marcus steps in. "Azalea, relax. OK? Let's just enjoy ourselves. I want you to relax. It's just me and you, OK?"

"OK, Marcus. You're right," Azalea says. Turning to the hostess, she says, "Let me apologize to you, Honey, for somehow offending you. I didn't mean to use common sense and confuse you!"

"RIGHT THIS WAY, please!" the hostess snaps angrily.

They sit down at the table and Azalea takes a deep breath as the hostess walks away.

"We are sitting in the perfect spot, Baby. So let's take a look at the menu, order some crab legs and shrimp, and anything else you'd like. This is your night. Just me and you."

"Oh, my! I can't believe it! Take a wild guess who's in next booth? It's Samantha and Edwin!"

"Oh, no! What are they doing here!"

"Azaaaleeaa!" hollers Samantha. "Hey, Girl! What you doing here! Is that Marcus? Oooooh, child, yes it is!"

"What's up, Marcus," Edwin says as he and Samantha join them at the table.

"What's up, Edwin! I thought yall were going back to Macon tonight?"

"Well, somebody got hungry and wanted to eat before we hit the road, so here we are!" Edwin says.

Samantha pops up from her booth and comes over to Azalea's side of the table. "Come on, Girl, let's go to the bathroom! We need to get caught up right now! Ooooh!"

Marcus looks up at Samantha. "Hey, why do women always go to the bathroom together? You don't see men inviting other men to the bathroom do you?"

Azalea smiles, shakes her head and stands up with Samantha. Marcus and Edwin begin a conversation as the ladies walk away.

"So," Edwin begins, "you starting to show your feelings for Azalea, huh? Ha, Ha. I've seen how you look at her. The way your eyes blink and you keep licking your lips before you talk. Who you think you is, LL Cool J?"

"Ha. Ha. Very funny."

"Alright, but not so fast," Edwin says. "Don't lose sight of our mission. Make sure you get invited to help her find her father's safety deposit box. Boy you good! Ha, ha, ha!"

"OK. OK. So it's like that, huh? You're trippin' on me. Ha, ha! Come on, you know me better than that. I'm a smooth operator! Ha, ha! Well, you know, it's been a *long time* since me and Janet were together, and Azalea, she's a nice girl. She's mature and funny, and I'd like to spend some quality time with her. Not to mention, she's inherited that nice piece of change, you know, from her father. Ha, ha! It's just perfect. We need the money to survive until we move to L.A."

"I wonder how much she got, don't you? That is the question. But, thanks to our little-big-mouth big-bird for spilling the beans . . . Ha, ha! Get them tipsy and they talk. Ha, ha!"

"You know it! All I've got to do is hang in there and we'll get our hands on that cheese. You know Azalea ain't got nobody, and now, she's got me!" Marcus says with an evil grin.

Edwin laughs, "Oh, we will hang in there. You just stick around until she finds that safety de-posit . . ."

"WHAT ARE YOU GUYS talking about?" Samantha says chipperly as she hops up to the table. "Us, I hope! Better be!"

"You miss me, Marcus?" Azalea asks coyly.

"Oh, more than ever. More than ever, Azalea."

"He, he, he," Edwin chuckles under his breath.

"You're *so sexy* when you laugh like that, *Mr. Edwin,*" Samantha coos. "OK. Let's order some food! Where's the waitress? I'm hungry!"

"I know that's right," Azalea says as she grabs a menu.

A waiter arrives at the table. "Helllloooo folks! My naaaaaaamee is Benjaaaamiiin," the waiter says in a sing-songy voice. "Are you ready to order? What are you good fellas having to drink? Let's start there and then I'll take your food order."

"In case you haven't noticed," Azalea says snootily, "these fellllllaaaass have dates! It's laddddiieess first and are you going to siiiinnnngg all night? I thought this was Red Lobbbbbbster not Broadway Tuna!" She says mimicking him.

"Wait a minute, lady, and mind your manners! I run this Red Lobster!"

"The only thing you run is up and down this carpet everyday because you work here. So, OK. Now, in case you don't know, you don't mess with two hungry, middle-aged black women!"

"It's not the women I'm worried about. Besides, Honey, Marcus and Edwin come here all the time with younger women, so that's why I asked them what they having this time, because trust me, *you're definitely on the menu,* but you're *nobody special.* Now, stuff that into your pillow and let it creep right into your dreams!"

"Woe! Dragon!" Azalea says angrily. "I'm going to add a foot up yo . . . !"

"WHY DON'T WE LEAVE?" Edwin cuts in sternly.

"No," Azalea snaps. "Why don't WE leave and YOU stay? We don't want the same V.I.P. treatment like ALL the other girls you bring here!" Azalea stands up and starts marching toward the door.

"Azalea! Wait! Wait?" Marcus calls out. "Don't leave. Let me take you home."

"No, that's OK. Samantha and I can ride together! So that won't be necessary."

"*We can?*" Samantha whines. "Girl, I'm waiting on my skrimps!"

"SAMANTHA! BRING YOUR BUTT ON! NOW!" Azalea demands, stomping her foot.

"Hey, Benjaney! I mean Benjee-men, can I get a boooooox to gooooo?"

No longer waiting, Azalea grabs Samantha's arm and pulls her out the door."

"Sorrrrryyyyyyyyy, Edwin!" Benjamin says boldly. "I did what you asked me. You gotta pay up. They don't act like dumb broads to me. $100. Pay up now, or I'm going to tell them you got me pretending like yall the regulars who come here often."

"Well, at least they didn't eat, so we don't have to pay for no extra food," Edwin says shrugging his shoulders.

"Is that all you think about? Money?" Marcus snaps.

"Right now, yeah. You know women, always getting emotional for no reason. Imagine if they was happy a few minutes ago and ordered. Do you know how much we was going to have to spend?"

"Probably not more than the $100 you owe the waiter! Oh, come on, man! I got to let Azalea know it ain't like that!"

"Well, call her. Holler back at her and let her know she still numero uno. And hang on in there, but just long enough until she find that safety deposit box. Ha, ha!"

"You wild. You wild and crazy, man. You so wild!" Marcus says with frustration.

Edwin begins to laugh.

Chapter Eleven

Back at the house, Azalea sits at the kitchen table with a paper plate and a box of fried chicken. "*Paula's Fried Chicken!* Azalea?" Samantha says rolling her eyes. "Me and you, sittin' in a funeral home, eating Paula's Fried Chicken when we could've been eatin' crab legs!"

"You can't go wrong with Paula's Fried Chicken. They may not have crab legs, but these chicken breasts make you forget about it. Don't nobody cook it like Paula. Well, except over at Ma Cora's. She has her own style. Now, that's my favorite!"

"OK, I love Ma Cora's too, but Girlllllllllllllll! Right now, I miss my order of dipped chocolate. Mr. EDWIN! Ooooooh, I miss him already!"

"Samantha, you're just getting to know him. It hasn't been that long."

Samantha takes a deep breath. "Girl, it feels like a week. He is so much fun. Never a dull moment. My soul mate. Azalea, you ever get that feeling with Marcus?"

"I don't know. I thought I was feeling something, but now I don't know what I'm feeling. I guess I don't have time to try and figure him out, 'cause, you know, the most important thing for me right now is to "handle my *father's* business."

"Girl, don't start quoting *them Bible verses* on me! Unless, uhmm, it's: *Ask and ye shall be given.* OK, so now I'm *asking* for Mr. Edwin! Mr. Edwin!" Samantha closes her eyes, sighs, then looks around as if Edwin were supposed to have magically appeared. "Girl, it ain't working!"

They both laugh.

"You forgot the other part of that scripture is *seek and ye shall find.* So just keep on looking!"

"Girl, give me a chicken waing. I'm having withdrawals!"

Azalea giggles as she pushes the chicken box toward Samantha.

"Samantha, we got some scavenger hunting to do."

Samantha's eyes widen and her voice lowers to a whisper. "Girl, that sounds so spooky. You know, saying that *in here.* A scavenger hunt—in a funeral home? Can't we call it something else?"

"Yeah, call it SCARED! OK, Samantha. Let's prioritize our thoughts. Let's not be so sensitive to disturb the *sensitive.* If you know what I mean?"

Inhaling a deep breath Samantha responds, "OK, Azalea. You know we're going to scare ourselves right out of this place, so be positive, OK? Let's talk about Mr. Edwin and Mr. Marcus, crab legs, Red Lobster, Paula's Fried Chicken, Ma Cora's cooking, but NO scavengers!"

"Now you making me upset. Why did you have to bring those creeps up again?"

"Maybe these spirits will go up to Mr. Edwin and tell him that it wasn't my choice to leave the restaurant . . ."

BAM!

A loud noise sounds from another room, and both women startle with fear.

BAM!

"Girl, you think the spirits taking us serious?" Samantha asks as she looks around.

"Will you shut up with all that crazy talk? There was no embalming in this building. This was my father's office and our family's living space. The bodies and all that stuff was done in the room that was off limits in the shed out back. The roof has fallen on that side, so I'm going to have them tear it down."

"Well, I would tear *all of this down* if I was you, Girl. Now, what was that noise?"

Azalea looks out the front window and sees the little newspaper boy riding away on his bicycle. She opens the door and finds the paper on the front porch.

"See, Samantha? That was only the kid delivering the newspaper."

"Girl, who reads the newspaper anymore? Most folks read online."

"I know, but I am supporting the little kid. You know, something to keep him on a positive path, especially since he said my father had an influence on him as a businessman."

"OK, let's make sure we do that, 'cause we don't want to disappoint nobody. You know what I mean, ah, no, um, don't want to disappoint no *body* in here!" She begins to look around at different parts of the ceiling, checking for ghosts.

Azalea watches Samantha, shakes her head and smiles. "BOO!"

~ *Change of Scene* ~

RING! RING! RING!

"Hi, Mama," Azalea says answering her cell.

"How did you know it was me? I wanted to surprise you!"

"Let's just say some of these *spirits* in my birth home told me, or maybe you can call it Caller ID? You know, Ma, I'm really starting to like this place."

"Your father was very proud of the funeral parlor. We spent a lot of nights in that place, just he and I together. Besides, nobody ever wanted to come see us, especially at night. He, he, he! That was always something I could count on, having just me and your father, alone."

"Well, Ma, sorry I came along and spoiled the fun!"

"Oh, no, child. I spent more time in Macon when you were born. You see, those lonely nights with John at the funeral parlor in Dublin is what got you here in the first place!"

"Oh, no more! TMI! Too Much Information, Ma! I don't want to get that picture in my mind, so please keep the rest of those secrets to yourself. Soooo, how you doin,' Ma? Are you OK being there in Macon all by yourself?"

"I'm never alone, Azalea. I've got God by my side at all times, and I've got Mr. Smith and Mr. Weston in the drawer! T. Sister stopped by the other day. She and those church ladies . . . They check on me a little too much! I was going to come down to help you clean tomorrow, but I've got to go to the court house, and to the bank to sign more papers. Now, I know that John didn't leave no debt, because he paid cash for everything, but I got a call from Marshall's bank across the river. They said I need to govern the account ASAP. I didn't know anything about this account, so I've got plenty to do right now!"

"OK, Mama. I'm on my way back to help you! It sounds a little strange . . ."

"Oh, no! You just stay right where you are and finish what you started, because you know . . ."

Azalea chimed in to finish her mother's sentence. Together they said, "That's the way Daddy would've wanted it to be."

"Bye, Mama. I love you."

"Bye, Baby and remember to lock those doors at night!"

~ *Change of Scene* ~

Azalea looked around the living room. She had finished cleaning and re-arranging the entire house.

"Now this is starting to feel like a place for the *living*," Azalea says to herself, feeling accomplished.

KNOCK! KNOCK! KNOCK!

Azalea startles. "Whoa! I better get used to live people comin' over. It's seems to be the norm. It really is starting to be a place for the living!" She murmurs to herself.

KNOCK! KNOCK! KNOCK!

Azalea opens the door. "Who-is-it?"

"Ma'am, I'm sorry but I must inform you that your grass service is going to be disc...ca...tinu....ded, and will not be cut because I have no payment."

"Do you have a name, or do you just like playing Knock-Knock, or something? First, you were the newspaper man, and now you the grass cutting yard man? What next? The window washing man?"

"No, Ma'am. My only other job is to keep my room clean and obey my elders."

Azalea smiles at the kid. "I'll pay you the money by the end of the week. You sure are a good businessman, and you've got good manners. Tell your father he taught you well!"

"I don't have a father," the kid says. "I have a foster parent, and I was taught business and how to respecting, I mean, how to be respect...ful of . . . to . . . other people by Mr. Johnson. I miss him. When is he coming back?"

"Well, I, I guess I kinda miss him too. I don't think he's coming back today though," Azalea says with tears starting to form in her eyes. "Run on home now. I'm sure your parent is looking for ya."

"Yes, Ma'am. I'll be back on Saturday to in...void, in…voicing your payment!"

"OK, you do that. You come back to see me with an invoice." Azalea smiles, shakes her head, and closes the door.

Chapter Twelve

"Alright, Macon's finest! Wake up!" The Police Chief ordered. "I want you to overdose on coffee because I need you to concentrate and find those crooks from Chicago! The last citing was 80 East. Who's got an update for us? Officer Johnson, you've been working this case. What's new?"

Officer Terry Johnson responds from his desk. "They flew down 80 East in stealth mode because no law enforcement spotted the vehicle from Dry Branch through Twiggs County, through Dublin, to Soperton, and beyond to Statesboro. So my analysis is that our little friends are hiding somewhere between Macon and Soperton, Georgia. Where? I don't know yet. I've downloaded and analyzed pictures of white vans taken on state emergency and neighborhood security cameras. Nothing is matching up."

"Alright. I am going to personally contact the Chief of Police and Sheriff in every city and county you named, beginning right now. Officer Johnson, I need you to get those pictures over to the widow, Mrs. Johnson. Wait a minute! Do we have a conflict of interest right now? Both of yall's last name is Johnson!"

"Same last name, different families," Officer Terry said in a dry voice.

"Well, good. I expect you to get her to identify the van from the pictures and then work to identify the suspects ASAP!"

"Chief, she's not going to be able to identify anyone, regardless of the pictures, sir."

"What you mean, Johnson? It says in your report that *you* got a statement from a Mrs. Johnson at that address. Come on! Everybody here already knows Mrs. Johnson at that address, so tell her not to be afraid to identify those thugs. Let her know that we're going to protect her."

"I understand, Chief, but the Ms. Johnson in the report is actually Mrs. Johnson's daughter, Miss *Azalea* Johnson. She is the eyewitness, but she no longer lives in Macon. Well, she sort of still stays with her mom some times, but she moved to Dublin a week ago."

"OK, Johnson. I'm contacting Chief Mitman at the Dublin Police Department right now. We'll work together and lock these hoodlums up before they pull their stunt again," the Chief says as he holds up his cell phone to his ear.

A few minutes later the Chief comes back to Johnson's desk.

"Good news, Johnson!" the Chief says. "I just got off the phone with Dublin Police Chief Mitman, and he says you're officially on the Dublin/Macon Special Unit. Make sure you go by his office and get sworn in! By the way, find that other Ms. Johnson."

"I'm on it, Chief! Seems like I've been thinking about her everyday. I mean locating her everyday, for the, ahhh, uh, for the report every day."

"That's the spirit, Officer Johnson! Obsess about it, and you're gonna find the one you're looking for."

"I hope so, Chief. I really hope so," Johnson turned around lost in thought. "*Azalea. Azalea Johnson. Where are you? Are you the one I'm looking for?*"

Chapter Thirteen

"This food is soooo good," a man with a husky voice says. He is sitting in a dark shed with another man and a woman.

"Either it's so good, or I'm starving," the second man said in a mid-tone voice.

"Well, it beats the cold cuts. It's not like we have a stove in this *rundown* shed! And she's a nice lady," the woman said.

"Did you tell her anything?" The first man with the deeper voice asks. "Does she know our real names? Listen to me, if you get to talking too much to that Chinese woman, I swear you'll never see Larry or Chicago again."

"I didn't tell her anything. I've done everything you asked me to do. I just want to go back home! Just give me the money you promised me to get my husband out of jail. For goodness sakes, he's your brother! You guys are pathetic!"

"Well, we can't do that right now," the second man said. "You know you're going to have to wait till we know the coast is clear before we let you go."

"And there's no way we're going back to Chicago right now anyway," the first man added. "They've got every cop and detective out looking for us. You don't just take a million dollars and disappear quietly. We are NOT going anywhere, anytime soon, so both of you just shut up about Chicago! And turn that flashlight away from the window. I don't want anyone to see us. There is somebody in that house up front. It seems like they moved in or something. We can't take any chances. If they see us, they never seeing any body again."

"But you promised nobody would get hurt!" the lady said defensively.

"Shut up!" The first man responded. "Nobody in *here* gets hurt! It's different for anybody trying to stop us. You do what we tell you to do if you want your share of this loot to get Larry out of the slammer! You do what we tell you to do if you *ever* want him to see the light of day again!"

"I'll do whatever you want me to do. Just don't hurt anyone, and please don't hurt Ms. Soon Lee. She's a sweet lady. My goodness! She is feeding us, no questions asked!"

"Why do you know her name?" The second man asked. "Soon Lee will be 'Later Lee' if she starts to get too friendly. Hmmmm. I want you to find out what she has in her house that we can use. We've got to move soon to a new location. This is becoming too close for comfort, and I don't like you getting too friendly with the locals. Get the food and keep your mouth shut!"

"Your brother would smash your head in for talking to me like that! How dare you!"

"Shut up, both of you! I've had enough!" The first man said. "We're gonna move *out* the folks who just moved in. We don't have much time and there can be absolutely no mistakes! Jessie, do what I tell you to do. You need to make friends with the new folks in that house. Me and Don gonna handle the rest. Shhhhhhh! I think I hear somebody outside. Get the gun! And no mistakes! Shoot to kill."

KNOCK. KNOCK. KNOCK.

"Mr. Johnson? Mr. Johnson! The lady said you wasn't coming back. I'm glad you came back. Mr. Johnson, it's me Alonzoe Tristen, from down the street. I can see your light. Mr. Johnson? Is that you?"

"Oh, it's a little boy," the woman named Jessie said. "What is he doing out here at night? I've got to open the door. He's just a child. Put that gun away. He's just a little kid! I won't let you shoot a little kid, Ray, I don't care how much money is on the line."

"Don, keep your hand on the trigger," the first man, named Ray, says. "If this is a setup, we gonna take 'em all out!"

"Open the door, Jessie. Open it slowly. Any funny business and this party is over!" Don says as he points his gun toward the door.

"Hold on a minute. Ah, I'm ah, coming to the door. Who is it?" Jessie asks loud enough for Alonzoe to hear her. Jessie cracks open the door and holds the flashlight out to see the little boy.

"Well, ahhhhh, hello! What a surprise seeing you here at night. What is a little boy like you doing outside this late? What is it you want, little one?"

"I want to talk to Mr. Johnson," Alonzoe Tristen said. "I can't sleep. The bogeyman wake me up again, and Mr. Johnson always give me a piece of newspaper to put on my covers for the bogeyman to read, and by the time he finish readin' I already be asleep."

"Well, ah, why don't you just use the newspaper you got from Mr. Johnson last time?"

"Well, Ma'am, the bogeyman already read that newspaper! Mr. Johnson always give me a new one for him to read!"

"Oh, I see. Well, we ain't got no newspaper, so go home, now! It's too late for you to be out here, and how did you know we, I mean, Mr. Johnson was out here?"

"I saw your light in the window from the street. Why can't I talk to Mr. Johnson? Why is Mr. Johnson using that flashlight? Is he looking for something secret?"

"Well, Mr. Johnso . . . " Jessie starts to say, but Don interrupts her.

"Scram kid! Ain't no Mr. Johnson here!" Don says as he walks over to the door. "You get yourself back home, and if you tell anybody you seen us, then we gonna send more bogeymen to your house and you'll never get any sleep! GET OUT OF HERE! RIGHT NOW!"

Alonzoe Tristen screams in fear, "Aaaaaaah! Why is everybody hiding Mr. Johnson from me? He is my men-tor. Mr. Johnson is a nice man . . ." The boy begins to cry.

"Don, stop it!" Jessie snaps. "You are terrorizing this child! Little boy, um, Mr. Johnson is not feeling well right now, but he told me to tell you to go home to your parents. I don't have any newspapers, but take this magazine I bought and keep quiet, and don't get no trouble started. That's what Mr. Johnson says to do. Go on now, and don't cry."

"Yes, Ma'am. I'll go home now. Thanks for the mag….agzine," Alonzoe says. He rolls the magazine and sticks it out of his back pants pocket, then jumps on his bike and rides off into the darkness.

"Now we got some serious trouble," Ray says. "Don, find out where that little nosey brat came from and burn down his house."

"Nooooooo!" Jessie screams. "We can't do this. Look at what this money has done to you! You are supposed to give me the money to get Larry out of jail, and that's it! Now, we are destroying homes, neighborhoods, and terrorizing little kids. I can't be a part of this any longer. Larry wouldn't agree to this!"

"You'll stay, and do what I say, or Larry will never see freedom again, and neither will you," Ray growls.

"Larry never broke any laws. He never committed any crimes. He is prison taking the blame for you two sorry brothers. I told him not to trust you!"

"OK, little lady! Enough Mary Poppins for one night," Ray barks. "Turn that light out now! Let's get some rest tonight and start all over again tomorrow."

Not knowing what else to do, Jessie obeys. She feels confused, and trapped as she turns off the flashlight, and stumbles toward her empty chair.

Chapter Fourteen

The next day, Jessie stood outside of the Piggly Wiggly grocery store talking with Ms. Soon Lee.

"Me happy you likee me cook-ee-ing. Tupper-ware, you keep. No need back."

"Yes, ma'am. We appreciate it so much. My brothers ate more than I did, but we all appreciate it."

"Welcome dear! You bringee you fam-ie for tea? I have recipes come down from my granny."

"Yes, ma'am. We'll do it sometime. As you can see, I'm always working, but maybe we can stop by soon," Jessie lied.

"Ab-so-lute-lee! You like town, you see. Welcome dear!"

"Thank you again. You're very kind."

"Oh, tank you muchee, dear! Funny ting, I no know where you from?"

"Up north, Ms. Soon Lee, but I'm beginning to love being in the South. The people are so friendly."

"Won-der-ful, dear! I see you family visit me, soon." With that, Ms. Soon Lee bows and backs away, walking into the grocery store.

"Well, hello, Ms. Soon Lee. How about some fresh produce today?" A clerk asks.

"You no play-ee with feelings, young man. I likee vegie-tables freshes!" Ms. Soon Lee laughs.

"Alright, Ms. Soon Lee. Ha, ha!" the clerk laughs.

"OK. I takee kale, red unyuns, potatee—ah—white potatee, six poun. Tank you."

"No corn this week?"

"Yes, tank you. I forgetee! Two ear."

"OK, Ms. Soon Lee. Why don't you enjoy your shopping and come back in 10 minutes. I'll have you boxed up and ready to go."

Ms. Soon Lee bows, then walks up and down the next two aisles as she collects groceries.

"Hello, Soon Lee," Mattie says as she walks up to the small elderly woman.

"Mottie! Oh, Mottie! So sorry John-ee gone! Good man," Ms. Soon Lee says.

"Thank you, Soon Lee. John always said 'Yes' each time you asked him to bury the homeless. You knew you could always count on John."

"Ob-so-lute-e-ly. Good man!"

"Perhaps a little too good sometimes. Soon Lee, I knew my husband *very well* and *always* made sure he was *well taken care* of at home. John was lacking for nothing!"

"No worry, Mottie. No ting between John-ee and me. You no worry. Me keep eye on him for you. John-ee good man in comm-un-ity. Only wishes I find him alive in garden that day. Gone too soon. He was pulling greens for food bank. So sorry, Mottie!" Ms. Soon Lee says as her tears begin to flow.

"Oh, you're right, Soon Lee. John was a good man in every town. Here, here's a hankie to wipe those tears," Mattie says as she reaches in her purse and pulls out a large white cloth handkerchief. "I am glad he was able to meet a member of the community like you too, and I'm glad he was a good neighbor to count on when you needed him the most."

"Tank you, Mottie. I get greens from John-ee garden back of parlor. John-ee plant veggie-tables, feed town rest of year."

"That's just fine, Soon Lee. I'll be in town for a few days, but Soon Lee, I don't want you to tell Azalea. I'm stayin' at a hotel. I couldn't sleep thinking about how much I miss John, so I came here just just to feel a sense of comfort. Sort of reliving some memories we had together in this town. Soon Lee, Honey, you missed the old days! Especially the night when I went into labor with Azalea! Did John ever tell you about that?"

"Mottie, John-ee alway tell-ee story. Never stop talking. I love listen his story. Over and over. But you no stay in hotel. You stay my house. You tell story again."

"Well, I don't know. Oh, Soon Lee, are you sure?"

Ms. Soon Lee bows her head reverently. "Yes!"

"Well, OK. OK. I'd like that very much but, we have to make sure Azalea doesn't know that I'm here. Soon Lee, I've been worried *so much* about her having to get the place back in order and then move here all by herself. My daughter is 43 years old and I'm talking about her like she is still a child! No matter how old she is, she's still my child, and I can't let go. I wanted her to be independent 'cause she didn't have no brother to depend on. I didn't mean for her to leave here for New York and be so independent that she never wanted to return. Oh, I wish I could let go. And really let her be independent."

"Mottie, Azale live in New York-ee all by selfie. She OK. Inde-pen-dent. She be OK."

"Soon Lee, could you follow me to the parking deck? I think its best I leave my car there for the weekend."

"Yes, Mottie. We go my home, make tea, talkee girl talkee."

The women smile, and head to the checkout counter.

Later that night at Ms. Soon Lee's home, Mattie sits comfortably at the kitchen table.

"Mottie? You OK? You at home? Comfort-a-ble? Spare room jus for you. No worry. Rest. Say long time. Not too long. Tea, Mottie?"

"Oh, thank you Soon Lee. I appreciate everything and I'm quite comfortable here. I looove those feathered pillows, child, I thought I was sleeping on a cloud a few moments ago during my nap. And, yes, I would love some more of that tea you made. I didn't know I would like green tea."

CHING-A-LING. CHING-A-LING. CHING-A-LING! A bell rings from the front yard.

"My goodness, what is that ringing out there?" Mattie asks.

"A-lon-zoe Tris-ten! Bike bell. Hope bike no stolen. Too late for A-lon-zoe be outside. Hope no bike stolen. Pity!"

Mattie peers out the window, but it's too dark outside for her to see anyone. The bell stops ringing. "Well, maybe he went home, or ran to the store for his parents or something. Besides, it seems dark, but it's only 9:30 right now."

"Mottie, A-lon-zoe no got parent. He live foster home. I no see foster parent. John-ee spend long time with A-lon-zoe. Teach be man. I no tell A-lon-zoe," she pauses, "No tell him John-ee no come back." Soon Lee begins to cry.

"No one has told the boy that my John passed?" Mattie begins to cry.

"So sorry, Mottie. No mean upset-ee you. Sorry, Mottie," Soon Lee continues to cry.

"Ooooh! Enough of this crying, Soon Lee! I'm so sad for the poor child. Certainly there's got to be something we can do. We've got to stay in his life somehow, and somebody has got to tell him that John . . ." Mattie is silent for a moment, then takes a deep breath and sniffles. "That John is gone. Poor child!"

"You right, Mottie. We tell soon, but we tell slow. Boy love John-ee much-ee."

"Telling that boy that my John is gone may be the most difficult thing I've ever had to do, but I've got to handle things the way my John would've handled things. He didn't believe in hiding things from nobody, except hiding money from me! Ha, ha, ha!"

Ms. Soon Lee laughs at Mattie's joke. "Ha, ha, ha! Yes, John-ee say you shop 12 hour one day, one store-e! Ha, ha, ha!"

"Honey, I sure did! He, he, he! John fell asleep sittin' in a chair in a fittin' room. He was holdin' his wallet 'cause I was 'bout ready to checkout. Instead of waking him, I just took the wallet and went on my way! Ha, ha, ha! By the time John woke up, the store had closed and he was asleep in the dressing room! I had to get the security guard to go in there, and get him out for me. I had already went home and forgot I left him there until I got to wondering why he wasn't there for dinner. Ha, ha, ha!"

"Ha, ha, ha! Funny, Mottie! Tell more story! Ha, ha, ha! Good laugh."

"Well, Soon Lee, let me tell you about the time John locked himself outside the funeral parlor, and had a funeral in one hour! That was about three years ago, before he took sick. Ha, ha, ha! I'll never forget. Everybody was just a'waiting on John to arrive at the church with the body. Honey, when I say it was a crazy day, I mean it was one of the craziest!"

The women laugh, enjoy their tea, and continue telling stories.

KNOCK. KNOCK. KNOCK. Someone knocks on the front door.

"Hello?" Ms. Soon Lee hollers from the center hallway. "Who tare?"

"It's me, Alonzoe Tristen, Ma'am, Ms. Soon Lee. I am deliver . . . delivery of your paper to you."

"Ah, tank you, Alon-zoe. I get money pay you. You want cookie? Two cookie? Favorite. Chocolate chip!" Ms. Soon Lee says with a smile.

"Ms. Soon Lee, it's not Saturday," Alonzoe says laughing. You forgot that Mr. Johnson showed me how to be accounting . . . I mean do my accont-tency . . . account-ing on every Saturday, at the end of the week. Today is Wed-nes-day!" Alonzoe Tristen says hesitantly.

"You right! Hee, hee," laughs Ms. Soon Lee. "You good business man. I pay bonus."

"Oh, thank very much, so very much Ms. Soon Lee, but I can't counting on my profiting . . . profit until Saturday, the end of week to keep my balance."

"Listen, Alonzoe, you and foster come to my dinners on Sunday. Make sure come you Sunday, Alonzoe Tri-sten."

"Soon Lee, is this the smart businessman who taught Mr. Johnson everything he knew?" Mattie asks, smiling, as she walks up the hallway.

"Alonzoe, say hi to Mrs. Johnee-son. Mottie, John-ee smart man, no need teacher."

"Hello, Mrs. Johnson," Alonzoe said politely. "Do you know Mr. Johnson? I've been waiting on him to come home because he helps me counting . . . count down my weekly money for my paper route and cutting grass. Ms. Soon Lee just gave me a bonus. Extra this week, so I can't count all that by myself!"

"Yes, I do know Mr. Johnson," Mattie's voice drops as she responds, "and we'll make sure that you keep up your accounting for this week. Why, Ms. Soon Lee and I know a thing or two about accounting."

"Well, OK, but Mr. Johnson tell me to always be three times as good as . . ."

Mattie unexpectedly joined Alonzoe in finishing his sentence. "AS YOUR BEST TRY!" they say in unison.

"Wow! Did Mr. Johnson tell you that too?" Alonzoe asked, speechless.

"Yes, Mr. Johnson told me a lot of things," Mattie said as she reflected. He told me about you, and let's just say, I am here to help you—just like Mr. Johnson. I would love to help with your accounting, and I promise, we'll be three times as good as our best try. In fact, I'll work harder than that. Would that be OK with you, Alonzoe Tristen?"

"Yes ma'am, I am thanking . . . thankful for you. Thank you, Ma'am, Mrs. Johnson. Thank you too, Ms. Soon Lee, for bonusing me. I mean, thanks for the extra bonus! I got to go to my next customer. It's paper time! Bye!" Alonzoe hops on his bicycle, and rides down the street.

"Mottie," Soon Lee called out, "You OK? You tell Alonzoe 'bout John-ee. I tink it break Alonzoe's heart. He young. He love John-ee," she said crying.

"I know, Honey. I will tell him . . . in due time . . . in due time, Soon Lee." The women walk arm and arm down the hallway back to the kitchen.

Chapter Fifteen

RING! RING! Azalea holds her cell phone to her ear as she waits for Samantha to answer her call.

"Hello?"

"Hello, Samantha. It's Azalea. I think I'm going to tear down the shed out back on the property, and renovate and sell the house. I don't really owe anything to this town and I don't need to be here either."

"Well, I think it sounds like somebody is preparing more work for *me* to do very soon, huh? As long as it's cool with your daddy, girl. I don't want no problems, nor do I want to somehow feel like he is asking me to leave. Girl, you know I'm still a lil' nervous when we change stuff around down there."

"Alright, Samantha! I hear ya!" Azalea laughs.

"Girl, you know I will help you try to convert wine to water, but please convert it back to the wine for me! You know I'm there for you. When do we get started? I got a lot of furniture in storage you can use if you'd like, you know, to set up the house so it will look nice to sell. Oh, this is going to be so much fun!"

"Slow down, Samantha! One step at a time. First we've got to clean that sucker out," Azalea says smiling. "We'll start Tuesday afternoon."

"Well, are you going to invite the Reverend to come over to go in there with us? You know, we might need an interpreter. Are you sure your dad finished the last funeral before he passed? I don't want to run into an old body or something. Maybe I can't do this, Azalea. I seen something like this on television the night before . . . Girl, how about I just make a donation?" Samantha laughs.

"Yea, you're gonna make a donation and you're going to help me clean that shed out! You know I can't trust anybody else out there except me and you, so we've got to get busy!"

"Well, we've got some more cleaning to do, I guess," Samantha says with resignation.

"BLEACH TIME!" The friends say in unison.

Chapter Sixteen

Officer Terry Johnson rides through a Dublin neighborhood in his unmarked police car. He's looking for Azalea's house, so he can find her and ask her about the the white van. He's not quite there yet, but he stops his car and gets out to help a little boy put the chain back on his bicycle.

"Hello. I'm Officer Terry Johnson. I'm a Police Officer and it looks like you could use a little help connecting that chain. Do you mind if I help you, sir?" He asks the boy.

"My name is Alonzoe Tristen, and thank you so much Mr. Official . . . Officer . . . *JOHNSON?*"

Officer Terry laughs, then picks up the bike, turns it upside down and begins to align the chain.

"Nice to meet you Alonzoe Tristen, but where are your parents? And why do you say my name like that? Do you know another Officer Johnson or something?"

"My frosting . . . fostering parent is home laying down on his bed. He say I can ride my bike, but I am confused, am confusing, because everybody moving here say their name is Johnson too. It's never been so many, lots of Johnsons, people named . . ." Alonzoe smiles and a laughs a bit, completely unaware of his speech impediment. "It is fun . . . funny to me 'cause I know the real Mr. Johnson. He is my mentoree, ah, m-mentor to me."

"Well, I guess that can be confusing, but sometimes people have *the same last name, but are from different families . . .*"

Officer Terry chuckles to himself. "Wouldn't Azalea get a kick out of this?" He says under his breath. He finishes putting the chain on the bike, and turns it back upright.

"OK, Mr. Alonzoe Tristen. Whew! Here ya go! She's like new again! Now you be careful, alert, and don't ride in the streets, OK?

And watch out for traffic. Sometimes some of us grown folks aren't paying attention, so don't put yourself in that situation, OK?"

"Yes, sir, Officer Johnson, but did you say *Ms. Azalea?* She live right down there at the end of the street. She got a shed back there. See, she live in Mr. Johnson house, but he ain't home yet!"

"Oh, well, Alonzoe Tristen, Ms. Azalea lives there because Ms. Azalea is Mr. Johnson's daughter. That's why she has the same last name. Ha, ha! And *Mr. Johnson?* Well, Mr. Johnson ain't comin' . . ." Officer Terry hesitates, dropping his head, unsure of what to say. "Uh, he ain't coming to the door, huh? Well, I'll ask Ms. Azalea about that and I'll let you know what I find out. So, how about that?"

"You mean I am detecting team now with you?" Alonzoe asks.

"Yes, I am making you a detective now," Officer Terry smiles.

"Oh, yes! I won't throw away . . . out . . . shout out . . . our cover. Thank you, Officer Johnson!" Alonzoe smiles really big, jumps on his bike, and follows Officer Terry as he drives to Azalea's house.

"Azalea?" Officer Terry practices as he walks toward the front porch. *"I hope you're ready to see me. I hope you're safe, and you're alright."* He begins to knock on the door.

KNOCK! KNOCK! KNOCK! KNOCK!

No one answers.

Alonzoe rides up, jumps off his bike, and leaves it in the grass as he runs up the steps of the front porch.

"Officer Johnson! Can I talk to you about something? Ms. Soon Lee inviting . . . invited . . . invitation . . . to me and my foster parent to her tradition . . . traditiation dinner on Sunday night. My foster parent can't make it because his body ache . . . aching bones. Ms. Soon Lee says I can come as long as I have a garden . . . guardian person in charge of me. Will you go be my guard person? Ms. Soon Lee cooks good hot food. She says it stick of . . . stick towards . . . in your stomach!"

"Well, I don't know if Ms. Soon Lee would appreciate that. She may be expecting your foster parent, and that's not me. I am a stranger here and good intentions don't always work out well amongst adults, so always report strangers to adults. Tell your foster parent that I'd like to meet him. Maybe I can help convince him to get up and go to Ms. Soon Lee's dinner. What is your foster parent's name, address, and phone number?"

"Do I have to tell you?" Alonzoe asks.

"I think its best. Adults need to have adult conversations, buddy! You're my ace, but somebody else is responsible for you, and that's who Officer Johnson needs to speak to."

"We live down the hill, at one of the shelter-assist homes. Do we have to go there now?"

"A good detective does his homework, right detective Alonzoe Tristen?" Officer Terry asks.

"I passed the fourth grade. I'm supposed to be in the sixth, but my test valuable-ation scoring was too low. So my teacher held me back and made me do fifth grade again," Alonzoe says.

"Those evaluation tests are ridiculous! Alonzoe, you're smarter than those tests! Get on your bike. I'm going to follow you to make sure you get home safely, and I'm going to meet your foster parent. What is his name?"

"Uncle Donald," Alonzoe says.

"Well, let's go find Uncle Donald."

Alonzoe Tristen jumps on his bike and cruises down a big hill, through a gated neighborhood into the assisted-shelter complex. Officer Johnson follows slowly behind Alonzoe. Once they arrive, he parks his car, gets out, looks around, and begins to walk to front door.

Alonzoe opens the door. "You can come in, Officer Johnson."

"Thank you. I'll just have a seat right here," he says as he sits in an overstuffed living room chair. Tell Uncle Donald I'm here to meet him."

"OK," Alonzoe says as he runs to the back room.

As he waits in the living room, Officer Terry looks around at the dusty furniture, old pictures, and empty water bottles, which are randomly scattered around the room.

"Officer Johnson, Uncle Donald says he would like to meet your quantity . . . quantinces . . . ac-quaint-ance too."Alonzoe stands still and stares at Officer Terry Johnson.

"OK," he answers, smiling, and waiting patiently. "This is a nice place Alonzoe Tristen," Officer Terry says as he impatiently fumbles with his hands. A couple of minutes pass and Officer Terry feels unsettled. "Alonzoe? Is your Uncle here?"

"Yes."

"I thought you said he wanted to meet me?"

"He does."

"OK, where is he?"

"He is in the bedroom. He can't walk unless the nurse helper lady brings him up front three times a week. He says he too heavy for me when I try to lift him up to bring him upfront to see the sunlight . . . shine . . . window time. If I keep practicing, I'll be able to pick him up soon and carry him to the front room."

"Oh, OK. Now I understand. You sure will lift him up, just keep working on it. Why didn't you tell me?"

"Because that is me and Uncle Donald's secret. If they know he can't walk no more, he say they take me from him."

"Oh, my. Well, let's go meet Uncle Donald . . ." Officer Terry begins walking toward the back room. Just outside of the bedroom, Officer Terry stops and turns to the small boy. "Excuse me, Alonzoe, let me have a private moment with your foster parent, OK?"

Alonzoe Tristen nods his head and waits in the hall.

"Uncle Donald, I presume?" Officer Terry asks as he stands next to the sickbed.

In a very faint voice, Uncle Donald responds. "Hello, you must be . . . Officer . . . Johnson. You make the kid think about ole man Johnson. He started looking out for Alonzoe when I got sick."

"Uncle Donald, do you know that Mr. Johnson passed away?"

"No. I didn't know. The boy didn't tell me," Uncle Donald says disparagingly.

"It's because he doesn't know," Officer Terry explained.

"I see. I can't look after Alonzoe no more. He's a good kid, but I can't do nothing for him. He is usually the one doing something for me." COUGH. COUGH. COUGH. "I haven't been outside in . . . years." COUGH. COUGH. COUGH.

"Uncle Donald, sir, you need to get to a hospital right now!" Officer Terry says.

COUGH. COUGH. COUGH.

"If I go to a hospital, they are going to take Alonzoe to another family."

COUGH. COUGH. COUGH.

"I'm the only family he knows. He is the son of my great niece who . . ."

COUGH. COUGH. COUGH.

". . . was killed by a drunk driver when he was only four years old."

COUGH. COUGH. COUGH.

"We come from a small family. All my brothers and sisters are gone. Only one had chil'en and Alonzoe is the only Tristen left."

COUGH. COUGH. COUGH.

"Please go with him to the dinner with Ms. Soon Lee. Tell Alonzoe about Mr. Johnson. I'll call my nurse . . ."

COUGH. COUGH. COUGH.

"And she'll take me to the hospital while the two of you . . ."

COUGH. COUGH. COUGH.

"Are at Ms. Soon Lee's dinner. Look after him for me . . ."

COUGH. COUGH. COUGH.

"Please do that for me."

Officer Terry Johnson nodded his head. "Yes, sir. I'd be happy to look after him at the dinner for you. I'm glad I got a chance to meet you, and I hope you have a speedy recovery. I'll bring Alonzoe Tristen to see you at the hospital after the dinner. Sound good?"

COUGH. COUGH. COUGH.

"That sounds good, but watch him for me . . . *Please*," Uncle Donald whispers.

Officer Terry nods his head, and then slowly walks back into the hallway where Alonzoe is sitting on the floor.

"Do you know why so many peoples . . . peoples and folks . . . say they have the same name like Mr. Johnson?" Alonzoe asks as he looks up at Officer Terry.

"I don't know, Buddy. Maybe Johnson is a very popular last name here in Dublin, Georgia. A few moments of silence pass and Officer Terry starts to speak again. "Well, I spoke to your Uncle Donald, and he says it's time for me to tell you about Mr. Johnson. Let's go into the living room and have a seat."

They walk into the living room and sit down on the couch.

"Alonzoe, did Mr. Johnson ever tell you what happens when a person goes to Heaven?"

"Ha! Ha! Ha! Officer Terry, you talking . . . speaking 'bout going to heavenly? Mr. Johnson always say he was ready, and told me to be ready too. He says I can go if I be good like him, but it's a long way from this neighborhood. I'm gonna save my savings to help get a ticket for Uncle Donald. He say he want to go there too."

"Well, Mr. Johnson has already left. He went to Heaven. And I'm sure that your good Uncle Donald won't need you to buy him no ticket. Do you know what happened to Mr. Johnson?"

"Yes, I know!" Alonzoe says laughing.

"OK. This is gonna be easier than I thought," Officer Terry says to himself. "Why don't *you* tell me what happened to Mr. Johnson. Take your time and be strong."

Alonzoe laughs. "Mr. Johnson is hiding in the shed! The lady with the flashlight told me when she gave me that magazine over there for the Bogeyman to read!"

Officer Terry skeptically repeats Alonzoe. "A lady with a flashlight? Alonzoe Tristen, I thought you said Mr. Johnson told you he was ready to go to Heaven?"

"He did say that. Is Mr. Johnson angry with me for accounting wrong? I want to talk with him. Why is he hiding from me in that shed?"

"Alright. Alonzoe, listen. Mr. Johnson has gone to Heaven like he told you. He is not mad with you or anyone right now. I'm sure he's pretty happy! But, if it makes you feel any better, I promise to go to the shed and see if I can somehow speak to Mr. Johnson, OK?"

"Thank you, Officer Johnson. There was a mean man who says he will hurt myself . . . hurt me, I mean . . . if I told anyone I saw him in Mr. Johnson's shed."

Officer Terry shakes his head and says, "OK. Thank you, Alonzoe Tristen. We're gonna stop the Bogeyman and all these other mean ghosts from bothering you. Will you let me borrow that magazine? I'll be back to check on you and Uncle Donald. Is that okay with you?"

"You promise?" Alonzoe asks.

"Yes, I promise. And trust me, I won't let you down!"

~ Change of Scene ~

Officer Terry drives behind Azalea's house and pulls up next to the shed. He gets out and starts looking over the front of the shed, which is in good shape. He then walks around to the back of the shed. The driveway is cracked and broken on one side.

As he turns the corner, he sees a vehicle covered with a tarp. He pulls the cover off and finds an old hearse. As he peers through a broken window of the shed, he sees a lot of dust, and odd pieces of furniture inside.

Turning around, he notices something large, covered with sheets and blankets. It's large enough to be a van. He pulls off one of the blankets finds the white van. Norest, Nevada tag number DAK369L.

Officer Terry immediately pulls out his gun, walks up to the door of the shed, and turns the knob to open it. No one is inside. He see the latest copy of USA Today lying on the floor. He puts on a plastic glove from his car, and bags the magazine and a few other recently used items as evidence. He pulls the white blanket back over the van, then quickly leaves the property.

~ *Change of Scene* ~

A few hours later, at the Dublin Police Department Police Chief Mitman smiles.

"Good job, Officer Johnson. The prints from the magazine you picked up from the kid belong to Jessie Dorman. She's the wife of Larry Dorman, who is already in prison. This has got to be the same family accused of swindling the widow out of a million dollars in Chicago!"

"Nobody was in the old building, and I didn't see any car tracks leading to and from it, so maybe they're walking, or maybe they hitchhiked out of town after dumping the van."

"Maybe, but maybe not," the Chief says. "The lab tech just emailed the fingerprint results from the USA Today you found in the abandoned funeral shack. The prints belong to a Ray Dorman. He's the brother of Larry. The Macon PD confirmed background info that both Dorman parents are deceased. There are three brothers left in the Dorman family: Larry, Ray and Don. I need you to stay on undercover detail, and find them. Watch their every move. find out how they are traveling back and forth off that property. I'll gather a backup team for a take-down!"

Chapter Seventeen

RING! RING! RING! RING!

"Herro? Azalrea? Is Soon Ree."

"Hello, Ms. Soon Lee," I know who you are.

"Oh! How you know?" Ms. Soon Lee laughs. "You on top of list for my dinner guest. You come and bring you friend help you clean. Sam-an-ta?"

"Thank you for the invite, Ms. Soon Lee. Yes, I'll be at your dinner, and yes, her name is Samantha. Trust me. She never misses a free meal! Ha! Ha! Ms. Soon Lee, truth is we both appreciate all of the meals you've dropped by this week. What would you like for me to bring to the dinner?"

"You no bring nothing. You come open heart, empty stomach. Ha! Ha! Ha! Special dinner. My treat. See you Sunday seven o'clock."

"OK. Thank you for thinking of us. I'll call my friend Samantha now. Goodbye, Ms. Soon Lee."

"Bye-bye, Dear!"

Azalea ends the call with Ms. Soon Lee and speed-dials Samantha.

RING! RING! RING!

"Hello?"

"Samantha! This is Azalea, girl! Heyyyy!"

"Hey, Azalea . . ." Samantha says softy. "How are you?"

"Samantha, I know that voice. I know that voice. That's the *woe is me* voice. What's wrong?"

"It's Mr. Edwin. He cancelled our movie date on Sunday night to go hang out with his *brother!* I was really looking forward to it. I was finally getting comfortable with him and was going to invite him over to my house. Maybe I was just too pushy or something."

"Come on, Samantha. You? Pushy? No way! Ha! Ha! Girl, just because he has to reschedule doesn't mean he doesn't like you. Maybe he does need to spend some time with his brother. Maybe his brother is going through something. Maybe Edwin is going through something and he's the one who needs to talk to his brother! It really doesn't matter because it's not about you. You're not the reason that brothers need to get together and bond sometimes. Anyway, that's why I am calling you. I just got off the phone with Ms. Soon Lee and she invited both of us to her family and friend's dinner on Sunday night. I already told her that you would most definitely be there too. Girl, so get your mind off Edwin and come on down to Dublin for some good food. I can't wait to tell you about the final plans for the property."

"Did you find the safety deposit box yet?"

"Girl, I'm talking on my cell phone inside of the Dublin Mall, and I really don't want to talk about that right now, but I've looked everywhere in that house and I can tell you there is no box!"

"Oh, Azalea," Samantha starts to whisper, as if the people in the mall might hear her voice. "Girl, don't tell me you have started some type of fight with them spirits in there for their treasure! Well, just tell the spirits they can keep the safety deposit box because we *don't* want to get all of them upset at one time. No! No! Especially not when I am on my way down there."

"Don't start, Samantha! Ha! Ha! I can't wait till you get here."

"I'll see you soon and phew phew on Mr. Edwin! Who needs that little short cricket anyway! Bye, Girl!"

"Bye, Samantha."

Chapter Eighteen

"What took you so long to get here today? You got off an hour ago. A kid can walk faster than that!"

"Don't start with me today, Don! I walked as fast as I could. I worked overtime, and Ms. Soon Lee insisted that she speak with me. Ray, I know you're not going to like this, but Ms. Soon Lee insists that she feed us dinner in her home on Sunday night. She says it's a family tradition, and it's an insult if we say no."

"See, I told you not to get too friendly with the locals," Ray said. "Now, there is some person out there who knows you, and knows you have "two brothers" who work all the time. I don't like where this is going, but I'm not going to let this stop me. We've got to get out of this town by the weekend, and we can't let this old lady get any closer, or any farther away from us. It's too late. Tell her we'd love to eat dinner in her home."

"No!" Jessie shouts. "Ray, you can't hurt this woman. She is so innocent. She hardly speaks English. She won't remember us. *Ray, please.*"

"Tell her we'll be there. What time?" Ray snaps.

Laughing happily, Don interjects. "Stop your whining, woman! If we get caught and go to prison, all of us are going. That means you too! It's your fault, making friends with the locals. Ms. Soon Lee this, and Ms. Soon Lee that!" Don laughs. "I can't wait to eat that meal!"

"What time we got to be there, Jessie? What time?" Ray demands.

"7 p.m. Jessie says softly."

"WHAT? Speak UP!" Ray shouts.

"7 P.M.!" Jessie screams, and then she begins to cry.

"Well, Don, we've got to get out of here next week. There is no way we can leave any tracks behind. Too bad for the ole broad, but let's raid her place and stock up our supplies."

"Yes," Don agrees. "Tell her we accept. We'll walk to her house the long way. We can't let anyone see the van. Tell her we'll get there around 6:45 p.m."

"I don't know when I'll see Ms. Soon Lee again," Jessie says. "I only speak to her when she stops by the cleaners on her way to the grocery store next door. She brings food for me and the rest of the crew working in the steam room. Ray, I'm telling you, there is no reason to harm this lady."

"What about that little brat on the bike? Did you find out where he lives?" Don snaps.

"No, Don. I've worked every day this week for nine and a half hours a day. And what do you guys do? Nothing! Absolutely nothing! You won't even use the cash you stole, for fear it will leave a trail! You make me work, and you do nothing! That little boy is harmless! I-won't-do-it! Let's leave. Let's leave now. Let's leave these harmless people to themselves," Jessie cries.

"Shut your mouth with all of the crying and whining. You've left us with no choice. Don't worry about the kid. He said he'll be back next Saturday to see somebody named Mr. Johnson," Ray laughs. "Let's make sure he talks to Mr. Johnson."

"What have I got myself into?" Jessie asks herself.

"FLASHLIGHT OUT!" Don orders.

One by one, the three turn off their flashlights. Jessie is the last to turn off her flashlight. Her vulnerable stare into the darkness expresses her dismay at the seemingly helpless situation. She sits in her corner, and covers her head with a blanket as she begins to shed tears.

Chapter Nineteen

"Hello. My name is Azalea Johnson. I want to speak with someone concerning a few home renovations and demolitions."

"Hello, Ms. Johnson. Thanks for coming in today," the woman at the counter says. "A representative will be available to speak with you shortly. We'll show you how to save money by using our construction company for all of your needs."

"Thank you. Please don't make me wait too long, OK?"

"Someone will be right with you," the receptionist says with a reassuring smile.

Five minutes later, a short, well-built man stepped out from a back office.

"Hello, Ms. Johnson. My name is Tommy Rodgers. I am the owner here and I hear you have a renovation project. I know you probably feel overwhelmed right now, but the process may be easier than you think."

"Thanks, Mr. Rodgers, and please please call me Azalea. Most folks refer to my mother as 'Ms. Johnson,' and I'm not quite ready to accept senior citizen status yet. Ha, ha, ha! I can't believe I'm actually responsible for whatever happens to this property. My father passed away and left me in charge of making these decisions. I wish my father would've sold the property many years ago! Well, I'm not sure what I really want to do. I'm torn between tearing it all down and renovating it."

"I'm sorry about your father. He was one of our customers for many years. He spent a whole lot of money buying supplies to help other people keep their homes in good shape. Mr. Johnson was a great citizen in the community, and there'll never be another person like him. If it means anything to you, I can tell you that he was a very smart man."

Azalea holds her head down as she clutches her cell phone. "Thanks, Mr. Rodgers. I needed to hear that, so I want to do whatever is necessary to update the property."

"Azalea, like I said earlier, your father was a very smart man. I don't know what your personal intentions are concerning your family's property, but I definitely look forward to discussing everything with you."

"Would you like something to drink, Ms. Johnson?" The customer service lady asks.

"No, thank-you for now, but I'll take a water-to-go, since its free. Ha, ha!"

"No problem, Ms. Johnson. I'll have a cold water waiting for you, Ma'am."

"Thank you, so much," Azalea replies smiling.

"OK, Ms. John—I mean, Azalea—I hope you're ready for this task today," Mr. Rodgers says as he holds a pen and an an armful of folders.

"Yes, Mr. Rodgers. I suppose I am ready. That's why I'm here. To handle my father's wishes."

"It's Tommy, by the way. You're going to call me Tommy if I'm going to call you Azalea. Deal?"

"OK. Sure. Deal."

"Speaking of your father's wishes, do you already know . . ."

Azalea interrupts. "Trust me, my first thought was to tear all of the property down and just make one big garden for the neighborhood, since they seem to love my father's gardening. But that's just it . . . my father's not here to garden anymore and I don't have any intention of keeping up the tradition. Mainly because I've got a blue thumb, and gardening is not one of my best trades!"

"That's no problem. You don't need any type of thumb. No green or blue one for this project. Do you already know . . ." Mr. Rodgers starts, but Azalea interrupts again.

"I'm not hiring anyone to keep it up either," she says. "Especially if I do all of this and the garden fails, so it's best for me to go ahead and tear down the shed, fix up the house, and sell the property. Do you know anyone interested in buying it?"

"Well, Azalea, you know I'm not a part of the decision making process. We're here to handle whatever you choose for the project and eventually I'll have to do whatever it is you want me to do, but do you already know..."

Azalea interrupts again. "Well, you see, my daddy wanted to remodel the house, and, unfortunately, fix that funeral parlor out back in the shed." Azalea continued to talk, acting as if she had a good relationship and kept in touch with her dad.

"Daddy, ah, yes he most definitely wanted to make sure the property looked good, you know add some shingles. I bet he'd like a clay tile roof too, and let's go ahead and look at your marble choices for floors and, yeah, ah, Daaaaadddy, umm, he wanted some granite counter tops and some new crown molding. You know Daddy liked green, so I feel like he wants me to accent the shutters in a mint green. Daddy liked colors you know?"

"No, I didn't know that. He always bought neutrals when he came into the warehouse," Mr. Rodgers says.

With a stunned, deer-in-the-headlights look, Azalea responds, "Oh? He did, didn't he?"

"Yes, so I guess you just answered the question you haven't allowed me to ask yet..."

"Question? I don't remember stopping you from asking me any question, Tommy. I make it a point not to interrupt people, I think."

"My point exactly. My question was, did you already know that your father, first of all, was a very smart man. In fact, did you already know that he left this folder for you. It already has your name on it?"

"Folder? No, I didn't know... You know Daddy loved to surprise folks. He was so clever," Azalea says laughing nervously. "Ha, ha, ha. You know, he should have told me about this folder last time I was visiting here."

"Well, it's been in our files for 17 years. Your dad came once a year. He and my dad were long time business associates. Mr. Johnson came once a year to buy supplies. He paid cash for everything. He donated the supplies to help repair homes of his less fortunate neighbors, though a whole lot of them were on different sides of town. Ha, ha. Mr. Johnson said everybody was his neighbor."

"I thought Mr. Rogers said that," Azalea joked. "You know Daddy definitely had a loud voice. He liked holding office and being on different boards." She lowered her voice to a whisper, "Now, this still a family secret, but you see Daddy was going to run for Mayor."

"Azalea, it seems we know two different people. Mr. Johnson refused countless nominations and request to hold all types of offices in this city. Truth is, Mr. Johnson didn't like the politics of getting along. He just liked to get along, so he donated and built things with his bare hands for folks all over this community. He definitely did it his way, and that was quite alright with the rest of the community because he was certainly a great man. My father and I enjoyed doing business with him."

"Well, I guess it has been seventeen years? People change. Thank you for the file, it'll be nice to hold on to some of his old stuff. Thank you for keeping family archives for me and my mother, old receipts, bills, and orders—a lot of my father's history. Can we talk about my plans now? How much is it going to take for me to demolish the shed and renovate the house?"

"One of the things that Mr. Johnson did every year was leave a different envelope with your name on it. Your father paid in-advance for the renovation project on your property. He voluntarily came in once a year and paid a cost of living increase for the changes in the economy. 17 years, what a man, what a man."

Azalea begins to smile, but then frowns. She looks confused.

Mr. Rodgers continues, "I don't know what his ultimate plan was for the renovation, but one thing for sure is that Mr. Johnson had already calculated his own estimates and left an order on file for all of the supplies, but I don't know what to do with it. He left this envelope for you."

"This is not what I expected today," Azalea says with a selfish tone. "I thought I was coming here to talk to you about my plans for renovating my father's property. Come on Tommy, more archives?"

"Azalea, listen to me. Your father already paid for the renovations. He left you a copy of everything in this envelope."

"Honestly, I was just wondering if you know if there is going to be any change left over once we tear down the shed?" Azalea says flippantly as she tears into the envelope. "Let me read this . . . What is it, a letter?" She asks with a puzzled glance at Mr. Rodgers.

Mr. Rodgers nods his head.

Azalea begins to read.

"Azalea, I don't want you to worry about any details of the renovations. I have already paid for them and I have written out my plans for the entire renovation . . ."

Azalea pauses, takes a breath, then continues to read.

"Mr. Rodgers has everything I've ordered in their warehouse and it will take six weeks to complete the renovations. It is my direction to demolish the entire property, which includes the house and the funeral parlor located in the back shed, and immediately begin construction on The Mattie Johnson Community Theater. I love you and always knew you would make it on the stage. How long will it take you to write your first play? Love, your father, John Johnson"

Azalea begins to cry.

"It's OK, Azalea. It's OK. When would you like for us to begin?"

Clearing her throat and speaking softly, she answers: "Saturday. NEXT Saturday."

"I and my crew will be there next Saturday morning at 7 a.m."

"Thank you, Tommy," Azalea says humbly.

Azalea quickly closes the file, wipes her eyes, and swiftly walks out the warehouse exit of Rodger's Renovation Services.

Chapter Twenty

"Soon Lee, let me help you with some of this work," Mattie says as she stands up from the table.

"Oh, tank you, Mottie. You no worry. You special guest."

"I tell you what, I will stay out of the kitchen and you stay out of the dining room for now. You tell me where to find your table settings and I'll take care of that for you. Trust me, I know how not to get in the way of the person in the kitchen! Besides, I'd really be in the way because I wouldn't know what to do to help you anyway. How many people did you invite?"

"OK. You helpie. Table setting in closet, end of hall. Set for ten peoples. You no in way. I love talkie cookie same time. Talkie help take mind off Azalea. You no smile big. You talkie, no worry."

"Well, I've got a table that needs my attention. So I'm going to set it while you finish cooking. We'll talk in a bit." Mattie starts to sing as she walks down the hallway. *I'm building me a home. I'm building me a home. Oh, my Lord! Oh, my God! What shall I do?*

Fifteen minutes later, Ms. Soon Lee walks into the dining room.

"Oh, Mottie! Table be-u-ti-ful! Tank you! So be-u-ti-ful, de-ar."

"Oh really, Soon Lee? I am so glad you like it. The food smells so good and everything looks lovely," Mattie says with a smile. She looks down, then drops her head. "It makes me think about Azalea and if she's eating, and taking the time to take care of herself. Maybe I did the wrong thing by not telling her that I am here. At least we could visit and she could talk to me."

Mattie starts to cry. "I'm sorry. I'm just worried about my grown child!" She shakes her head and smiles. "Ha, ha, ha! I used to hate it when my mother did that to me! Whooo! Ha! Ha! And now, I understand exactly what my grandmother meant when she used to tell my mother, I don't care how many years you get under you,

you still just a child to me! Ha, Ha!"

Ms. Soon Lee stands still, watching Mattie, and listening.

"My Grandmother used to stay on my mama," Mattie continued, "and my mama would stay on us, especially the girls! No! No! You are going to be a young lady in my mother's presence. Oh, these young parents these days are too liberal. I don't see how any parents let their twelve-year-old girls wear those shorts cut all the way up to their buts! We have to take back responsibility for the village! We need to reach in and teach the mothers at the same time as we are teaching the children because that's the root of the missing link. I know there are lots of single mothers out there, but if we teach our daughters how to be independent women, we won't have to worry if they can handle tough situations on their own."

"Mottie, you no need worry. Azalea grown, in-de-pen-dent. You say you taught her be in-de-pen-dent. She OK. You no worry!"

DING-DONG! The doorbell interrupts Ms. Soon Lee's train of thought.

"Oh! First guest here. Early!"

DING-DONG!

"Soon Lee, are you saying I don't count now? Since you're calling the folks at the door your first guest? Hee, hee!" Mattie jokes. "You've already thrown me away!"

"No, Mottie. They friends. You family. You sit next next me. You get com-for-table, and you no work now. Sit. I get door."

Ms. Soon Lee walks to the front door, opens it, and invites her guests in. "Wel-come. Wel-come," she says with a bow. "These your brothers? Handsome!"

"Hello," Ray says. "It's a pleasure to meet the lady who opened her home to us for dinner tonight. I'm really looking forward to an enjoyable time here tonight."

"Ms. Soon Lee," Don says with a laugh, "Ha, ha, ha! Seems like I already know you and now it is such a pleasure to meet you . . ."

Jessie interrupts, "Ms. Soon Lee! Me and my brothers are very glad to be here."

"Wel-come! Follow inside. I takie you to dining room. I introduce you my dear friend."

"*INTRODUCE?*" Ray asks surprised. "What? You mean more people gonna be here too? Jessie, I thought you said she invited us to dinner, not to *a* dinner!"

"Oh! Dis annual friend and family dinner tradition. I lonely old lady, but gots mor tan tree friends. Ha! Ha!"

"Well, the more the merrier, Ms. Soon Lee!" Don says with a grin as they all follow her into the house, down the hallway, and to the dinning room.

"Mottie," Ms. Soon Lee calls out. "Dis is nice lady from cleaners I tell you 'bout."

"Well, hello young lady from the cleaners! I'm sorry, child, but I didn't catch your name?"

"Hello," Jessie says smiling. "My name is . . ."

Ray interrupts her, "Excuse me, but does anybody know how to get to the bathroom?"

"Down hall-way, turn righ' and firs door on righ' is bat-room," Ms. Soon Lee explains. "Jessie, you and brothers sit chairs on left of table."

"Well, I'd like to sit by you Ms. Soon Lee," Don says with a laugh. "Ha, ha, ha!"

"Ooh!" Ms. Soon Lee smiles. "A bodyguard! I like! Ha, Ha, ha!"

"Ladies first, Don!" Jessie snaps. "Remember your manners in Ms. Soon Lee's home."

Mattie begins to stare at Jessie and Don, unsure of the vibe she feels.

"Thank you for letting me use your bathroom," Ray says. "How are you ma'am?" He says as he turns toward Mattie.

"Mottie is sweet friend, won-der-ful. Visit me few week," Ms. Soon Lee says.

"Hello," Mattie says with a smile. "What did you say your name was?"

"I didn't say. We just met, lady. But my name is, uh, Arthur. Arthur Hancock."

"It is nice to meet you, Honey," Mattie says with a motherly tone. "It's nice to see brothers still hanging tight with their sister at your age. Soon Lee tells me how hard the two of you work all week to take care of your sister's financial needs too. Hmmmm, what a wonderful family. Have a seat with the rest of your family, Arthur."

"Oh, Ms. Soon Lee," Don pipes up. "It sure smells good in here. I'm getting hungrier by the minute."

"Ha, ha! Hot food come up soon, so just sit and make self at home," Ms. Soon Lee says.

"I'm gonna do just that, Ms. Soon Lee! Just that!"

"Would you like some sweet tea, Honey?" Mattie asks Jessie.

"Sweet tea? What's that?" Jessie asks.

"Oh, my, my! Y'all must be from up north somewhere? Sweet tea is southern for the words sweetened tea."

"What is it sweetened with?" Ray asks.

"Oh, sugar of course! Ha, ha!" Mattie says as she looks curiously at the trio.

DING-DONG! DING-DONG!

Ms. Soon Lee takes a peak back down the hallway to see who is at the front door. "Mottie, dear. You still want help Soon Lee?"

"Why sure, Soon Lee. I told you just let me know anything I can do to help you."

"Oh, tank you, dear! Bring joy! You go front door. Wel-come guest. I go kitchen. Last dish al-most rea-dy. You mind, Mottie, dear?"

"Soon Lee! Ha, ha! Of course not. It would be my pleasure. Excuse me y'all. I'll be right back." Mattie stands up from her seat at the table and slowly walks down the hallway to answer the front door.

DING-DONG! DING-DONG!

Outside, the next guests stand on the front porch.

"Samantha, quit ringing Ms. Soon Lee's door bell like that! She has excellent hearing! Give her a second."

"I am glad to know that, because my kidneys are about to explode!"

DING-DONG! DING-DONG!

"Come on, Ms. Soon Lee!" Samantha says as she crosses her legs.

The door begins to open slowly.

Before the door is open, in unison Azalea and Samantha call out, "Hello, Ms. Soon Lee!"

But it isn't Ms. Soon Lee answering the door.

"MAMA?! Oh, my goodness! Mamaaaa!" Azalea cries.

Mattie throws both hands up in the air in complete surprise. "Oh, Azalea! I am so glad to see you child! I've been thinking about you everyday!"

Mother and daughter hug, and Ms. Soon Lee shows up at the door smiling. She bows at Samantha and then backs into the house.

Samantha pushes past Mattie and Azalea in a hurry to find the bathroom.

"Down hall-way, turn righ' and firs door on righ' is bat-room," Ms. Soon Lee explains to Samantha.

"Mama, how you been?" Azalea asks. "I kept leaving messages on your cell phone and I got worried when you haven't returned any of my calls."

"Baby, now you know your mama don't know how to check them messages on that phone. I keep that thing for 9-1-1. It's number one on speed-dial. Ha, ha, ha! I knew you called, Honey. I just didn't want to lie to you and not tell you that I was already here. I wanted it to be a surprise."

"Mama, you and that cell phone! Ha, ha, ha! You won't change and you'll still have that same one for the next ten years. Ha, ha, ha!"

The women hug again.

"I love you, Mama and I'm so glad you are here with me because now I know everything is going to be alright! You know why? 'Cause my mama is in-the-house!"

"Ha! Ha! Come on, let's go eat," Mattie says laughing at her daughter. "Soon Lee has been so excited for her family and friends dinner today! She has really put a lot of love into that kitchen! I need to see if I can help her with anything. Azalea, you're sitting right next to me on the right side of the table."

As they walk into the house, Samantha comes out of the bathroom and meets Mattie and Azalea in the hallway. They enter the dining room together and see Ms. Soon Lee arranging dishes on the table.

"Ah! Azalea, Sam-an-ta, dis is Don, Arter, and Jessie. Don, Azalea Johnson is Mottie's daughter. Single. Pretty!" Ms. Soon Lee says with a bow before darting back to the kitchen for more food.

"MARCUS?" Azalea yells out, shocked.

"And this is Arthur, Arthur Hancock," Mattie says pointing at Ray.

"Ray, ooops . . ." Jessie slips.

"Why are you here? How are you here? Arthur? Ray? Don? Who are you?"

"Mr. Edwin!" Samantha exclaims as she rushes to Ray's side. "How did you find me? This is sooo romantic! Oooh, Mr. Edwin, my heart was so heavy! I knew deep down inside you didn't mean to abandon me! I forgive you! You're so romantic! Ahhhh Mr. Edwin? But, who is *this lady?*" she says pointing to Jessie.

"My name is Jessie, and I work at the cleaners next to grocery store. That's where I met Ms. Soon Lee, and these two are my . . . brothers!"

Don (Marcus) interrupts, "FRIENDS!"

"Brothers," Ray (Edwin) says dryly.

"I'm still going to fix your plate for you, Mr. Edwinnnnn, or whatever your name is! You're probably a secret agent, aren't you? Oh, my very own James Bond!"

"Get a grip, Samantha!" Azalea says gritting her teeth. "Sit down! Something's not right!"

Ray (Edwin) jumps up and says, "Yea, why don't everybody have a seat right now. I think we need to talk and *really* get to know each other."

"Azalea, who is this Marcus and this Edwin y'all talking about?" Mattie asks confused. "I knew y'all was too close for brothers and a sister, and who ain't never heard of sweet tea? The last person who asked me about sweet tea was my cousin from Chicago. Are y'all from Chicago? Oh, excuse me, please! I think I'll go help Soon Lee bring out more food." Mattie rolls her eyes and starts heading to the kitchen.

"I don't think she'll be needing any more help from you, old lady!" Don (Marcus) says to Mattie.

"That is my mother, Marcus! Don't talk to her like that!" Azalea yells.

Don (Marcus) stands up with an intimidating stance. "Marcus? Ha, ha, ha! Azalea, you'll fall for anything! I don't care if she is your mother. We said for everybody to have a seat!"

"Mr. Edwin, you going to let him talk like that to my friend and her mother? You need to let him know how to talk to ladies. Show him how to be classy, like you."

"Classy? Like who?" Mattie says in disbelief.

"Mama! Not now!" Azalea mumbles under her breath.

"EVERYBODY SIT DOWN!" Ray (Edwin) screams as he pulls out his gun and starts waving it around. "Take a seat, because you might as well consider this your last supper."

"Ray, you promised!" Jessie pleaded as everyone sits down at the table.

"So Ray, it is, huh, Edwin? Or is it Arthur? You'll never have a real person in your life because you don't even know who you really are!" Samantha snaps.

"What does it matter now, Samantha? You've told me everything about you that I need to know, and now you know just a little too much about me," Ray says coldly as he pulls out a gun and points it at Samantha.

Samantha starts trembling and talking really fast. "Did I ever tell you I had a memory condition? I can't remember anything past five minutes ago. Do I know you, SIR?" Looking at Azalea, she says, "And who are you, young lady?"

"Samantha! Get a grip!" Azalea says. She takes a deep breath and calmly turns toward Ray. "OK. So, ah, Mister whoever you are, let's talk this over. We've got some property we can give you. I'll go sell it, and it and bring you the money."

"Oh, no you don't!" Mattie says as she crosses her arms. "John wouldn't allow these thugs five minutes onto his property!"

The group hears Ms. Soon Lee shouting from the kitchen, "I be in with last dish so we can eat!"

Samantha, Mattie and Azalea all start to stand up and say, "I'm gonna help in the kitchen!"

"You see, it's a part of Ms. Soon Lee's tradition," Azalea says pretending to be in authority. "All of the women must help in the kitchen right before the last dish comes out. Ah, see it's good luck for all of the women to touch the last pot. Jessie, girl, you need to go with us. This is a special . . ."

Don interrupts, as he pulls out his gun and points it at Azalea. "SIT DOWN! It's gonna be bad luck if any of you ladies move a muscle from this table."

"Make room for dessert on table!" Ms. Soon Lee shouts. "I coming now. It hot!"

"I'm warning all of you, don't try any funny business, or the ole broad gets it when she walks in here!" Don says. He and Ray hide their guns under the edge of the table cloth.

"OK! Every-ting hot and ready! Tanks for being guest to-day. Each you make dis day so special. I want my friend, Mottie, please say a prayer, dear."

"Ms. Soon Lee, didn't you forget the tea? Let me go get it for you!" Samantha says.

"Tank you, dear, but I leave tea on pur-pose. There no room for it here. Tea fresh when pour in cup. Last part of tradition for family and friends dinner."

"Well, I'll go check the temperature on the stove to make sure it's hot enough . . ." Samantha continued.

"HEY!" Don snaps. "The tea is fine! Have a seat!"

"Oh! You hungry man, huh?" Ms. Soon Lee asks Don. "No testy. Come, Mottie. Say prayer. We eat."

Mattie stands up to pray, "Ooooh, JESUS! Please show up and show out! I'm asking you to pay a special visit to each guest here today. I mean every single one of them too, and judge us by our deeds! Bless the . . ."

"OK! We get it!" Ray says. "Take a seat!"

"Yes, Mama, please sit down! And Lord, please answer her prayers!"

"OK! Dig in. Stay as long as you like. Enjoy foodie!" Ms. Soon Lee says.

DING-DONG! DING-DONG!

Everyone stares at each other, unsure of what to doo next.

Samantha sees her chance, "I'll get it!"

"No, Sam-an-th! Sit. Eat! I check door," Ms. Soon Lee says as she walks out.

"You heard the woman. Everybody dig in," Ray orders, "because this is going to be one long night!"

Down the hall, Ms. Soon Lee opens the front door.

"Well! Alonzoe! So glad you make it, dear! And now I meet foster! I knew must be good man in smart boy's life. Handsome too! I Soon Lee. I happy you here, my home."

"Thank you, Ms. Soon Lee, for invitationing me to be here. I am glad I could make it, and this is my guardian . . . guardian nation . . . person responsibility for me! I'm sorry to tell you, but Mr. Johnson won't be here like last year."

Ms. Soon Lee looked a little surprised that Alonzoe knew Mr. Johnson wouldn't be attending. "You right. Mr. John-son no here," she says as she looks down at the boy's hands. "Why you bring rope? You no have belt?"

"This is the rope Mr. Johnson gave me to keep it on my bicycle," Alonzoe explained. "He says you never know when you're gonna need . . . emergency time . . . emergency."

Officer Terry laughs. "Seems like Mr. Johnson taught him just about everything he knows. And some things he won't let go of. Hello, Ms. Soon Lee. My name is Terry, and I'm glad to meet you. Thanks for having us in your home, and I hope you don't mind the rope. Alonzoe, why don't you hang it on the door?"

Alonzoe begins to wrap one end of the rope around the inside handle of the front door. He ties a slip-not around the handle, and hangs onto the other end, letting the rope drag behind him. "OK, but it is my responsible . . . responsive-ability to keep up with the rope. I promise it won't get in the way, Ms. Soon Lee."

"You no worry. Rope OK. Careful, no trippie! You need it to pull you from table. You belly 'bout to be full! Ha, ha, ha! Now, follow to dining room. You meet other guests," Ms. Soon Lee says as she bows and waves Alonzoe and Terry into her home.

Officer Terry's phone begins to ring as they walk down the hallway. "Oh, I'm sorry, Ms. Soon Lee, but I need to step outside and check this message. It's a very important phone call. I'll be right back."

Officer Terry heads back outside as Ms. Soon Lee ushers Alonzoe into the dining room and into a chair.

"Meet special guest Alonzoe Tristen! You take seat next to Ms. Sam-an-th. I get you chocolate chip cookies to eat with meal, dear."

"Hello, Alonzoe Tristen! It's so good to see you," Azalea says. Turning to stare at Don and Ray, she adds, "This is a kid, and this kid has been through enough already, so early in life."

Smiling brightly, Alonzoe Tristen says, "Hello!" to the group.

"Hello cutie! Come on over here and sit next to me," Samantha says. "As a matter of fact, I'm going to get you a fluffy pillow to sit on! Excuse me y'all."

"I'm not going to tell you anymore to SIT DOWN, woman!" Ray barks.

"You are a mean man!" Alonzoe Tristen says to Ray. "You shouldn't be talking to a lady like that. Mr. Johnson say that's disrespecting . . . disrespect-full to womens folks."

"I thought I already told you to keep your mouth shut, you little rotten kid!" Ray says.

"Wait a minute, whatever your name is," Mattie says as she lifts her butter knife from the table. "If you lay a hand on that child, you're gonna draw back a knob!"

"Ole lady, you just chose yourself to be the first example to pay the cost of being a hero," Don says to Mattie.

"Wait a minute!" Azalea exclaims. "My mom, she doesn't mean any harm! You know how old school-parents are these days. They fear nothing, but they speak way before they understand what they're saying, and in this case, who she is saying it to."

"RUN, ALONZOE! RUN!" Jessie says.

"Hello everyone!" Officer Terry says as he walks into the room.

"Why, you sure look familiar! It is you! Off . . ." Mattie begins.

"No, Ma'am. I don't think so," Officer Terry interrupts her quickly, winking. "I've been told that I have a familiar face, and I meet a lot of people. I sell insurance. So maybe it is me, or maybe NOT?"

"Oh, no! Azalea, we are not allowing no other man to lie to us!" Samantha butts in. "Officer Terry Johnson! Now, you know we've met before! Don't you remember when we was at the O.S. Club in Macon a month ago?"

"I'm sorry, Ma'am, but we don't know each other," Officer Terry says winking.

"You can stop it right there! Azalea, Girl, he is winking at me! This is not a time to flirt! Maybe later?" She adds.

"Samantha!" Azalea cries, "Listen, the *nice man* has never met us before. This is our first time meeting him, OK?"

"Oh, Azalea, the stress is too much for you. You're losing it. You're in denial!" Samantha says.

"Pipe down, woman," Ray says. "And you listen, Mister. Have a seat, right next to ME!" Ray stands up and points his gun, this time at Officer Terry. "So, you are an Officer?"

"No, he is not!" Samantha says as she rubs her eyes. "My contacts slipped again. I was seeing double! Ha, ha, ha! He looked like a twin. I'm so sorry Mister. Can I go get you something to drink?" She stands up as if to go to the kitchen.

"SIT DOWN!" Don says as he stands up and pulls out his gun.

"OK. OK. You got me," Officer Terry admits. "I'm a cop and I can't lie. Thanks, Samantha."

Mattie rolls her eyes at Samantha.

"Yea, thanks Samantha," Azalea says.

"Oh, my goodness, Ray! I told you we should leave this town! I can't be a part of hurting these good people," Jessie says with a whine.

"Take me and let them go," Officer Terry says.

"Come on, y'all. Let's go!" Samantha says jumping up.

"MS. SOON LEE!" Don yells. "We need you to come on out of the kitchen right now!"

"COMING!" Ms. Soon Lee yells from the other room. "Just few minute more and Alonzoe's cookies finish."

"Listen," Officer Terry says to Don, "I know people who can make a deal to help you straighten out some of your problems. Don't take this moment and make it worse. What do you say we work on it?"

"No dice, pig. You know we're going to go straight to prison," Don says. "Deals don't work where we're from, unless *we* make the deals, and right now, there is NO DEAL!" He says as he slams his fist down on the table.

"Well, in that case, you leave me no choice," Officer Terry says.

Alonzoe Tristen ducks beneath the table to hide.

"Don't be a hero. There's no way you gettin' out of here!" Ray warned.

"You're right," Officer Terry says, and then he yells, "NOW!"

From under the table, Alonzoe reels in the rope he brought, which pulls open the front door. Chief Mitman and the Dublin Police Department's take-down squad rush inside the house and down the hallway with their weapons drawn.

"Don't you two move an inch!" Chief Mitman says. "I promise you won't know what hit you if you do!"

The rest of the officers take the guns from Ray and Don, immediately putting them and Jessie in handcuffs and escorting them out of the house and into the back of a police van.

"Good job, Officer Johnson! I'm glad we got the tracking dogs on their scents earlier because you were right once again. All the tracks led here."

"Well, Chief Mitman, the hero here is Alonzoe Tristen. Good job, detective!" Officer Terry says.

"Yes, good job, ah, detective!" Chief Mitman adds. Staring at Alonzoe, the Chief whispers to Officer Terry. "Officer Johnson, did you get the message I left for you on your cell phone earlier? Did you tell the kid?"

Officer Terry shakes his head, "No."

"I see," the Chief says. "Why don't you enjoy the rest of your evening? We'll take care of everything from here, and I will definitely file a good report with the Chief at the Macon PD. You know, I could use another smart man like you around here. I wish there was a way to convince you to stay. Think about it." Turning back to the rest of the group, he says, "Sorry, everybody, to disturb your dinner, but our job here is done!"

Alonzoe Tristen is busy talking to Mattie. "Mr. Johnson say I can be brave at any aging . . . age!"

"Oh, and I can tell you that he is so very proud of you today," Mattie says smiling.

"All the way from Heaven?" Alonzoe asks.

"Yes! All the way from heaven."

Ms. Soon Lee finally walks back into the dining room. She is carrying a plate of hot chocolate chip cookies.

"Alonzoe! I cookie you cookies! But I burn, so I makie some more from scratchie. I add 'lil iceie cream on top. You special guest. Ha, ha! Oh, you lookie like you see ghost! You OK?"

"Well, if he didn't, I SURE DID!" Samantha says. "May I use your restroom again?"

"Oh?" Ms. Soon Lee says as she looks around the room. "Where Jessie and brothers go? I take long time in kitchen. They leave before dinner startie? Must be very hungry."

"It's OK, Ms. Soon Lee. They won't get hungry any time soon." Officer Terry says. Turning to Azalea, he says, "I think I'm going to stay in Dublin as long as you want my help, and then some. Now that I've found you, I'm not planning on going anywhere anytime soon."

"Terry Johnson? I thought you said we just met? Ha, ha, ha!" Azalea jokes. "Thank you for everything."

"Azalea Gwennamore Johnson!" Mattie exclaims. "You are blushing. Oh, how sweet!"

"Time to eat!" Ms. Soon Lee adds.

The group sits down and begins serving, and passing the food bowls around the table.

Chapter Twenty-One

Judge Allenwood sits behind the bench in the Laurens County Courthouse. "Alonzoe Tristen," he begins, "do you understand what is going on here today? Today is a very special day that affects the rest of your life. I have seen you go through so many changes in this community since you were a little baby.

"I knew your grandfather, Bernard Tristen. He and I were classmates, like you and your friends. Sometimes, life can be difficult for all of us. Nobody has a perfect life, nothing is perfect, but I am very glad today to add more happiness and completion into your life. Are you ready for the next phase of your life, young man?"

Alonzoe Tristen gives the judge his widest smile. "Yes your honor-able, honery-honor!" The representative from the state's foster care program straightens Alonzoe's tie and nudges him to stand up straight in front of the Judge.

"Ha, ha, ha! I haven't been called ornery since my late wife gave me that name. First of all, Alonzoe Tristen, I hereby present you with the reward money of $100,000 for catching the thieves who stole the widow's money in Chicago." The judge leans forward in his chair to eye Alonzoe. "Can you count that high yet, son?"

"Yes, sir. I learn counting from Mr. Johnson before he go to Heaven."

"Oh, that's good! You deserve this special day because you earned it the old fashioned way. You worked really hard at being a smart student and a model citizen for other young people in the community. Do you know that all of the other little kids are looking up to you? You are a role model now."

"I am? I thought I had to have other folksis to be role modeling. I didn't know I could be a role model too, your honors, sir."

"Oh, yes. Mr. Johnson was a good role model to you, and now you must be a role model to others, but wait—there's more! There is absolutely no way this court can turn over $100,000 to a juvenile, so it will be put in a trust fund until you are 21-years-old. It will pay for your college education, and other needs at that time. Additionally, starting now, the interest earned on the funds will be paid to you in a monthly payment for your living expenses, like clothes, shoes, and a shiny new bicycle. Now, this leads me to the next phase of the hearing today. You know these nice people from the state juvenile protection office want what's best for you, and we've got to place you in a loving home."

"Did I do something wrong?" Alonzoe asks, confused.

"Of course not," Judge Allenwood says. "Officers, please open the door. Sir, please approach the bench, state your name, and your pledge to this court."

"My name is Officer Terry Johnson, and I pledge to this court to . . . to be the best father for this smart, brilliant, young man. Your honor, I pledge to provide a loving and safe home for Alonzoe Tristen for the rest of his life, until he becomes an adult, and decides to move out on his own.

"My door, and my heart will never be closed, your honor. I petition this court on this day to legally make him my son! A young man needs a father, and, a lot of times, a father needs a son. I pledge today to this court that I shall protect and guide him to continue to become a more productive citizen in this community. So help me God." Officer Terry took a deep breath after he finished his pledge.

"By the power invested in me as Chief Justice in this Superior Court of Laurens County, I hereby grant you full custody and all parental rights of governance and responsibility of Alonzoe Tristen-Johnson! Good luck to both of you!"

TAP! TAP! TAP! The Judge beat his gavel on the bench.

Alonzoe Tristen Johnson turns and looks at his new father, Officer Terry Johnson. Officer Terry turns to look at his new son.

"Son, come on here! Let's go home!" Officer Terry Johnson throws his arms around Alonzoe Tristen Johnson, and they jubilantly walk out of the court room.

Chapter Twenty-Two

"Samantha, I am so excited! Only a few more days until demolition begins on the shed out back—the old funeral parlor of the property! My father was certainly unselfish. All of this time, I thought he wanted me to run the funeral home, but he only wanted me to be me! My father is building me a community theater! I am still in shock and disbelief! Oh, but I am so happy! Thank you, Daddy!" Azalea says looking up to the ceiling.

"Mr. Johnson," Samantha says, also looking up to the ceiling. "Please don't answer with *you're welcome!* Azalea, if you don't call him up, then maybe he won't show up anytime soon. At least wait until after I'm gone. Ha, ha, ha! You know we've got a lot more work to do 'round here. What time is Goodwill coming to get all of this furniture?"

"The Goodwill folks are arriving at 1:30 today, and my mother and Ms. Soon Lee are bringing some volunteers. We've decided to keep a portion of the property for the community garden. Terry promised to help replant everything. He says he'll keep the garden in good shape. We'll have this neighborhood back up to code in no time. You should see Alonzoe Tristen. He is one happy kid now!"

"Hey, that's Alonzoe Tristen *Johnson* now!" Samantha corrects Azalea. "Look how God works! Looks like everybody is getting some happiness in their life," she says. Her smile slumps into a frown. "Well, everybody, but me."

"Oh, Samantha! Just slow down and let that man come to you. You have a lot going for yourself. You're professional, beautiful, and you have a great personality! Samantha, you are my best friend and I want the best for you. You have no reason to feel less than worthy. You're incredible."

"Thank you, Azalea. You're my best friend too. You know there's nothing I wouldn't do for you."

"Good! Because Tommy Rodgers of Rodger's Renovations and Demolitions, and his entire crew will be here on Saturday to tear down the shed. But we've got to go through it first."

Samantha's eyes stretch wide open. "Girl, you took my words too seriously! I will do anything for you EXCEPT go out there in that shed—funeral parlor—or whatever you want to call it! I don't think me and you ought to be the persons to go in there. You know, those ghosts and bodies were there first, and some of them might still be hanging around, but I don't want them hangin' 'round me!"

"Samannnnntha! Stop it! Ha, ha, ha!"

"I will help you, only for you Azalea, but never ask me again! You and Officer Terry Johnson are really hitting it off. Hey, why don't you ask him to come over and clean out that shed—parlor—with you? Ha ha!"

Azalea rolls her eyes.

"I would have never put the two of you together," Samantha continues. "He was so fat back in school, but he is a good man. Finally, my friend has someone that truly loves her."

Azalea smiled and took a deep breath in. "It seems like we've been together a long time now, but, yes, yes, Samantha! I am so happy and Terry puts me in the right place in life. He is such a gentleman and he makes it a point of doing something special for me every day. I just don't know how Alonzoe feels about all of this. I hope my relationship with Terry doesn't disturb his happiness with his new father."

"It won't," Samantha reassures Azalea. "Alonzoe, he is a good kid. He understands, but I guess any kid being around is an important reason to be hesitant in this new relationship. All three of you are experiencing something new with each other."

"You're right, and I am sensitive to the boy's happiness and his needs in terms of having a father. Terry is the father Alonzoe has spent his little life searching for. He is the father that assures him of his presence, understanding, and support. And Alonzoe looks up to Terry. He really respects him. Their bond is mutual. It's a relationship like I never had with my father."

KNOCK! KNOCK! KNOCK!

"Samantha, get the door! It must be the volunteers that my mother secured to help replant and soil the community garden. Finally, it's becoming a reality!"

"Oh, Girl, I'm gonna learn how to be domesticated! I want to plant some of those yellow things that come on a stalk—whatever you call them."

"CORN?"

KNOCK! KNOCK! KNOCK! KNOCK! KNOCK! KNOCK!

"Wow, you got some impatient volunteers, Azalea." Turning toward the front door, Samantha shouts, "Hold on a second! I'm coming!"

Samantha opens the front door and is immediately engulfed by a pair of outstretched arms.

"Well, hello, Baby! It's Meeeeeee! T. Sister!"

Samantha struggles to breathe in the midst of T. Sister's humungous bear hug.

"Help!" Samantha chokes out, but no one heard her over T. Sister's shouts of joy.

Chapter Twenty-Three

Ms. Soon Lee, Mattie, T. Sister, and the church ladies work together to soil and replant the community garden. Azalea, Samantha, Officer Terry Johnson, Alonzoe Tristen Johnson, and other friends are also working in the garden.

Suddenly, several trucks drive a convoy through the neighborhood and park right in front of the shed—parlor. One-by-one, the volunteers in the garden stop working. Everybody walks to the parlor-shed and gathers together to witness the kickoff of the property demolition.

"Hello, Azalea! How are you today? Me and my guys will have this building torn down in four hours. You won't have any memory it was ever here."

"Oh, my! I don't know if I can take it," Mattie says. "Everything my John worked for comes down in four hours? John never spent four hours on any project here. He gave it a lifetime." Her tears begin to fall.

"Mottie," Ms. Soon Lee says, wrapping her arm around Mattie's waist. "You come work garden. It better for you."

"Oh, Mama. I'm sorry, but this is what Daddy wanted me to do. Remember the letter?" Azalea asks.

"Child, I don't need *no* letter to explain what your Daddy had planned for you. I always knew." She pulls a letter out of her apron pocket. "Your father wrote two copies of that letter each year with his own hands. One for the old Mr. Rodgers, and the other one for me. Azalea, you see, those were our plans together for you."

Mattie walks arm-in-arm with Ms. Soon Lee back up front to the community garden.

Tommy Rodgers pulls out a large sledgehammer from his truck. "Azalea, here is a sledgehammer. Why don't you take the honor of delivering the first swing."

"Yes, Azalea! It will be therapeutic for you," Samantha says. "Just take that sledgehammer and let it rip!"

Azalea holds the sledgehammer and looks around at everybody.

"Yea, Babe! Go for it!" Terry says.

"I'M READY!" Azalea shouts. "WE'VE GOT A COMMUNITY THEATER TO BUILD!" She lifts up the sledgehammer, throws it over her shoulder and slams it directly into the outside wall of the shed—parlor!

BAM! BAM! BAM!

She hits the wall three times.

The wall begins to fall apart as it caves into a big hole. Suddenly, cash money begins to spiral down out of the top of the hole, flying all over the place!

"Oh, my goodness, Azalea! It's the safety deposit box!" Samantha laughs and screams.

"Oh, my goodness! The safety deposit box! Oh, my goodness!" Azalea screams excitedly.

"Looks like your father was truly old-school if *that wall* is the safety deposit box!" Terry says.

Everybody begins helping Azalea collect the cash. Alonzoe Tristen Johnson tries to count all the money, but he is confused because there is so much he can't keep up. The church ladies are smiling, cheering, and celebrating!

"Girl, give me that hammer and let me knock down a wall!" Samantha says. "You know, Mr. Johnson might have a wall with some hundred dollar bills stuffed in it! Oh, excuse me, Mr. Johnson, but I do want to say thank you for the walls!" Samantha says, looking up to the sky. She turns to Azalea, "We're cool now," she explains. Samantha grabs the sledgehammer, but is barely able to lift it, much less swing it over her shoulder.

"Hey," Tommy Rodgers says. "Would you like a regular hammer?"

"What am I going to do with a regular hammer? I'm trying to knock a wall down! Don't you see all that money flying around? Are you kidding?"

"I thought maybe you were kidding—especially since you're trying to lift the sledgehammer from the wrong end."

"Oh! Why don't you show me how to lift it? I'm on a mission. You see, I want to go ahead and knock down my wall before *they* think about coming in my direction."

"They?"

"The dead," Samantha whispers, as if she doesn't want them to know she's talking about them.

"Oh, I see." Tommy Rodgers says. He moves to stand behind Samantha. "Well, first of all, you need to grab the handle to pick it up." He places his hands over her hands and continues, "Like this. Now, let me see you do it on your own."

Samantha, appearing traumatized, slowly moves her hands over his hands, "Like this?"

"Now you got it, but why don't you stop by our Info Center at the Warehouse? My staff will show you the safe way to use tools, saws, and machines. My name is Tommy, and you are . . . ?"

"Samantha Diane Brantley! I'm a Pisces, and I'm only pretending to be forty-two years old."

"He, he, he! Well, I am forty-two years old," Tommy Rodgers says.

"I'm forty-two. Really am, forty-two. Yes, I am forty-two. Really, forty-two, too," Samantha says, jumbling up her words.

"What are *you two* doing over here?" Azalea says as she steps around the corner of the parlor-shed. "Ooooohhh!"

Officer Terry Johnson follows quickly behind. "Yeah, Tommy. You get lost? Ha, ha, ha!"

"Ha, ha, ha! I'm sorry but I wanted to make sure this beautiful lady doesn't hurt herself."

"Trust me, she will make sure of that!" Azalea says.

Everyone laughs.

"I don't think Daddy has any more money in these walls," Azalea says. "Honestly, I don't think my daddy would set me up to be on a scavenger hunt. He always made it easy for me. I didn't realize it back then, but I do now. There is nothing else in these walls. You may go ahead and tear it down."

"Girl, wait!" Samantha says. "Give me a few minutes to run over here and knock around the bathroom window. You know how you get a feeling when you think you're gonna win the lottery? I got that feeling now. Give me five minutes."

"No, Azalea is right," Tommy says. "There is nothing else in these walls."

"You mean you knew about the money in the walls too?" Azalea asks.

"No, we didn't. But after we thought about it and completed an analysis, we figured his safety deposit box had to be in the front left wall."

"How did you figure that out?" Azalea asks.

"Yea, you say you didn't have any clue?" Officer Terry Johnson adds.

"Well, in all of the years of handling business with Mr. Johnson, the front left wall was the only part of the funeral parlor he never had us remodel. He always handled everything concerning the front left wall. Ha, ha, ha! I told you, Mr. Johnson was a very smart man!"

"*And so are you*," Samantha says.

"Thank you, and perhaps when you come by the warehouse, I'll *personally* teach you Safety Tools 101," Tommy says to Samantha. "Now, everyone, I'd appreciate it if all of you stepped back over there about 500 feet for a few minutes," he says pointing toward the garden. He holds up a work bag and hands it to Azalea. "Pick out a pair of safety glasses and watch us do the dirty work! Azalea, do we have your permission to begin?"

"Let her rip, Tommy!" Azalea shouts. "LADIES AND GENTLEMEN! LET HER RIP!" The demolition trucks converge on the shed and begin to completely tear it down.

"I can't believe I've spent the last night ever in that house, my birth home. I somehow feel complete and whole again. Especially with you in my life, Terry," Azalea says.

"I've got some good news, Babe. Today, I transferred to the Dublin Police Department under Chief Mitman," Terry says. "My first day is Monday, so now I don't have to drive back and forth to Macon everyday, and I won't have to stop early anymore when we're working in the community garden, or the community theater. I want to be here. I am going to be here to support you. I've got your back. I'm proud of you, and I can't wait until you finish writing your first play. I'm going to be Chief of your set design team. Whatever you want me to do, I'll do it. You can do it. We can do it!"

Azalea melts into Terry's arms as he embraces her in a big hug.

Chapter Twenty-Four

"How do you turn the channels on this here digikal TV set?" Mattie asks Azalea.

"Mama, its digital. You don't have to turn the channels anymore. Ha, ha, ha!"

"Well you better get me straight before you have company. Do you remember that time when I kept trying to change the channels with that old garage door opener? Keep all of those gadgets away from me! Baby, you got so many remotes in your house, I don't see how you keep up! Set the channel for me on that station that's playing *Touched by an Angel* back-to-back."

"Mama, that's called a marathon."

"You can't tell me about *Touched by an Angel!* Roma Downy and Della Reese! They ain't got nobody racing on that show! They do turn into that little white bird and fly around. It look like the same bird to me, so I ain't never knew if Della and Roma both in the same bird, but that's another story! Set the TV on that channel."

"Mama, you are so funny. You know those were doves, and who you think was sitting there watching the same show with you? Me!"

"I love this new house you bought. You remind me of your father. You got lots of land, but what made you want to move all the way out to the county?"

"The land, Mama. I'm glad you love it here too. I remember riding past this land with Daddy when I was a child and he always said how much he loved this property. The peace and quiet offered me the perfect place to finishing writing my first play. I can't believe tonight is opening night for my play at *The Mattie Johnson Community Theater!* I'm getting nervous!"

"No need to get nervous! You've done all of the hard work. The rest will come easy for you. Just stand up there and let your heart speak for you. When you hear your heart speaking, then make sure you answer! I'm so proud of you, Azalea. Your Daddy would be so proud too! Tonight is going to be a special night!"

"Thank you, Mama," Azalea said with tears in her eyes.

Chapter Twenty-Five

Later that evening, everyone gathered for opening night at *The Mattie Johnson Community Theater*. Mattie, Ms. Soon Lee, and city officials cut the grand-opening ribbon and made speeches about John Johnson and his dedication to the community. Now, it is Azalea's turn to speak about her play, her father, and to thank the cast.

Holding a microphone on a stage surrounded by the cast from her play, Azalea began. "I want to thank the entire community for your support. It was such a beautiful moment to see so many hands working together to beautify the neighborhood. You did it—we did it!

"Tonight, we opened *The Mattie Johnson Community Theater!* It's a place for the arts, dance, music, and galleries. It's a place right here in Dublin, Georgia, where we display national exhibits as well as debut works by local and regional artists.

"I want to thank God for watching over this entire process. I want to thank the woman whom this theater is named after: *The Mattie Johnson Community Theater*. Standup, Mama!"

Mattie smiles, stands up and waves to the sold-out crowd of citizens filling the theater.

"I want to thank Ms. Soon Lee for her overwhelming support. She has been the glue that keeps us together. I want to thank Alonzoe Tristen Johnson, who truly is my father's protégée.

"Thank you to Tommy Rodgers and good folks at Rodger's Renovations and Demolitions who understood my father's wishes for a community theater. They built it to exact perfection!

"And to my best friend, Samantha. You never left my side. I don't know how I would've made this journey without you, Samantha. I love you, girl!"

From her seat in the audience, Samantha screams out, "I would like to thank the Academy as well as the Foreign Press for this Grammy . . ."

"Shut up, Samantha!" Azalea says, and everyone in the room laughs. "Thank you all for coming tonight." Azalea looks up toward Heaven, breathes in, and says, "AND, this moment would not be possible without the man upstairs who sent me my Daddy."

She begins to cry as she continues, "Daddy, you always allowed me to have a happy childhood. I never knew a sad day when I was with you. You allowed me to feel grown up and go chase my own future on Broadway in New York City, but who knew my path would lead me right back to this stage tonight in Dublin, Georgia? Daddy, you have made my fondest wishes come true, so your love will forever be celebrated here at *The Mattie Johnson Community Theater!* YES! YES! YES!"

The entire building erupts in applause. "Thank you for your support and good night to each . . ."

"HOLD UP! Hold up! Excuse me! Wait a minute! Azalea, please excuse me, but I want to say something!" Officer Terry Johnson interrupts as he and Alonzoe Tristen Johnson make their way through the theater to the stage.

"Pardon, excuse us, please ma'am, and lady, people and gentle sirs!" Alonzoe says as they quickly walk to the stage, passing between all the cast members.

"Azalea, I'm sorry, but may I hold the microphone? There is something I want to say to my new community."

"Why, sure . . ." Azalea says, dazed at what was going on.

Officer Terry Johnson grabs the mic and looks at the audience. "Thank you for accepting me into your community. My life is almost complete. I've met some wonderful people in Dublin, Georgia. I've gained a son for life, and, and I've fallen in love with a *wonderful woman . . .*"

Azalea is smiling. She is proud of Officer Terry Johnson and Alonzoe Tristen Johnson.

"Can I get somebody to hold this microphone for me?" Officer Terry asks. "I get nervous in front of large audiences and my hands are shaking! You would think its three degrees up here! Ha, ha, ha!"

Alonzoe Tristen Johnson grabs the microphone. "I got it, DAD!"

Suddenly Officer Terry Johnson grabs his kneecap, seemingly in pain. The audience reacts with a, "Ooohh!"

"Are you OK, Baby? T. Sister is here!" She shouts from her front-row seat.

"Oh, I'll be alright. I'm sure I'll be alright," Officer Terry Johnson says as he holds his knee and bends down while rubbing it."

"Terry, you want some of these strong guys from the cast to help you get up? Let them help you. Are you okay?" Azalea asks.

"Yes, Azalea. I am OK. In fact, I've never felt better!" He pulls out a small box while he is down on his knee. "And yes, you can help me. *Azalea, will you marry me*?" He asks.

Azalea throws both hands in front of her face, as she is overwhelmed with emotion. The audience applauds!

"Same last names!" Alonzoe shouts.

"One family," Officer Terry Johnson says as he stares deep into Azalea's eyes. "One family." He opens the box and pulls out a 5-karat engagement ring that once belonged to his great grandmother.

"Azalea, will you marry me?"

The End

Acknowledgments

The process of writing a book is a journey full of challenges, hope, and personal fulfillment. It is quite different from my everyday world of radio and entertainment; however, I've enjoyed the creative experience of this new opportunity.

First of all, I want to thank God for the gift of allowing these characters to run around in my head since 2002.

I want to thank God for my grandmother, Lizzie Tillman, who helped raise me along with my six brothers on Simmons Street in Dublin, Georgia.

I want to say you to Mrs. Martha Green, my English teacher at Dublin High School. She taught me the beauty of reading by **insisting** that I keep an open mind by reading an entire book before placing any type of judgment, stereotype or summary because of reading something offensive.

I also want to thank Mr. Roscoe Brower, my Industrial Arts teacher at Dublin Junior High School. He unlocked my potential to become a quick writer by encouraging me to run for the office of Secretary at the annual state conference of the Industrial Arts Convention. I was elected, and the experience changed my world. By encouraging me along the process, he embraced a fatherless child as his own son and taught me many things about being a young, positive black man. I will forever refer to him as "The Greatest Role Model of All Time!"

I want to thank my "Uncle Bud," Barnabus Relaford, for literally giving me the keys to his laundry mat during my summers on Ogeechee Road in Savannah, Georgia. He convinced me that my dream of being a business man would come true one day.

Thank you Rachael Hartman, my editor and publisher at Our Written Lives, for allowing me to share my personal goals and for helping me reach them by taking me through the publishing journey step by step.

Special Thanks and in Memory of Mrs. Thomasenor Pearson

Mr. Carl Pearson and the Pearson Family of Dublin, Georgia for being my backbone when my back was against and through the wall. Carl Pearson is one of the smartest brains in the world. His family (Mr. Alfred Pearson, Sr., Ojetta Pearson, Alfred Pearson, Jr., and Herbertta Pearson) gives more to the community than they'll ever receive or seek in recognition. Thank you for being a true friend since childhood, through my college days, and now in adulthood. You are simply the best!

To those who truly support me in the creative productions and ideas that I've been fortunate to share. Thank you for allowing me to be uplifting in your life.

Thanks to Family and Friends

To my beloved children: Aja Lasha Chatman Hall and Kenneth Barlow. Wow, time flies! Suddenly both of you are full grown adults! I love you. And to all of my seven grandchildren, I love you all and I want you to set your goals high, and spend the necessary time to reach them!

My Brothers: Bishop A. Tim Chatman, the first Black Police Chief in Dublin, Georgia, and his wife Verlinda; Terrance Chatman; James Chatman, Sr., and his wife Dr. Theresa; Andre Chatman, and his wife Felicia.

Thanks to my Aunt Camilla Allen, Aunt Rebecca Harris, and Aunt Ethel Spikes, to my uncles, nieces, nephews, cousins, godchildren, neighbors, and those whom I adopted along the way as a part of my life.

Thanks to Alonzoe Kyler for taking the photographs for the cover of the book, as well as my author photos.

Thanks to my God-sister, Katrina Relaford, for being my cover model.

- Genola "Mama Gen" Burke, my second mother
- Angela Collins
- Florene Brown, my other mama
- Auntie Betty Lou Denson
- Margaret Hughes and Evelyn Brown, my babysitters
- Mrs. Bessie Bailey
- Mrs. Vera Smith
- Mrs. Ida Bell Moss
- Mrs. Jessie Holliman
- Mrs. Julie Driger
- Mrs. Dornetta Beard-May
- Edwin May
- Chris Brown
- Mr. and Mrs. Ernest and Lucille Wade
- Mrs. Deborah Callaway-Bargie
- Marilyn Moore
- Bernard (JUKE) Brown and Brown Family
- Rudi Redding
- Ed Denson
- Kaye Plummer
- Kemonde Lindley
- Tijuana Swint
- Rhonda Timmons
- Rita Hall
- The Spikes and Kyler Families
- Brenda Jackson
- Annie Hutchinson
- Ruth Henderson Hubbard
- Wylene Hardy
- "Ma" Christine Walden
- Artis Thomas
- Earline (Ms. Dab) Wallace Appling
- Kenny and Robin Brazil
- Mrs. Sandra "Pinedale" Allen

- Nerita "Mini Me" Davis
- Sebastian "DSouth" Riley
- Diamond "The Queen" Young
- Pierre "Ovadose" Nelson
- MY SIP FAMILY
- Shirley "Mama Mea" Harris
- Arlinda Garrett
- Kevin Fox
- Kim Jordan Fluker
- Chancansco (DJ Skillz) Tolbert
- DJ Wiz
- Annette "Queen B" Watson
- David Booker
- Cassandra "Ms San" Curry
- Allen Davis
- The MVP Band
- James "Revy-Rev" Harris
- Antwon Little
- Hamp "King Bee" Swain
- Linda Dupree Key
- Bobbie Lowther
- James Isaac
- Rick Humphrey
- Yvonne Lamb Castillo
- Wanda Maxine Relaford Beckett and The Relaford families originating from Riceboro and Savannah, Georgia
- The entire Simmons Street/Allenwood Drive/Plummer, Ray Street, Telfair Neighborhoods in Dublin, Georgia
- All those associated me through my radio, TV, and print publishing careers!

Thank You For Being You!

In Memory of Those Who Helped on this Journey

Mrs. Pauline P. Moss
Mrs. Catherine Martin
Mrs. Rosa Curtis
Mrs. Linnie Bell McGirt
Sister Zelma May
Cousin Mary Etta Woodum
Ray "Satellite Papa" Brown
Charles "Big Saul" Green
Pastor Joseph Foston, of the Wabash Street Church of God
Stacey Renardo Chatman & Gregory Bonoski Chatman, my brothers!

About the Author

Derrick "DC" Chatman was born and raised in Dublin, Georgia and graduated from Dublin High School in 1982. His family environment was full of music and creative arts. He is one of seven sons raised by their mother, Cora Chatman Smith, on Simmons Street in Dublin. Derrick enrolled in Morehouse College in 1982 as a Business Administration major.

He began his radio career at WQZY Y96/Dublin in 1989. His main focus was advertising and creating the hugely popular, "Derrick Chatman Show—The Soul of the City," which was the only black music radio station during the late 80s to mid-90s in that area. During that time, Arlinda Garrett chose Derrick Chatman as one of her protégées to help market Master P's music and other projects in Central Georgia. That opportunity launched his career in the record promotions arena.

In 1994, Derrick Chatman joined 97.9 WIBB/Macon where he became the youngest Station Sales Manager in history of Macon radio. In 1995, he created "DC's New Artist Profile Radio Show" that launched the careers of DJ Skillz, Young Dro, CMD Styles, Sonny Spoon, and many others. He was blessed with many great opportunities including interviewing President Jimmy Carter, President Bill Clinton, James Brown, Little Richard, and many others.

In addition to 97.9 WIBB in Macon, throughout his career DC worked at WMSU in Starkville, Mississippi, WQVE in Albany, Georgia, and WGXA Fox 24 in Macon, Georgia. He also wrote a bi-weekly entertainment column in the 11th Hour Music Magazine, and served as the national host of Herschel Walker's National Talent Competitions across the country.

He is the proud owner of DC Productions Entertainment and Southern Mecca Records. He is excited about the release of his first book and the completion of his website to expand his brand of entertainment, publishing, and promotions.

Our Written Lives
book publishing services
www.owlofhope.com

9 781942 923183